in medias res

Latin term for "in the middle of things." Starting a story in the middle at a crucial point, rather than at the beginning, and filling in background information as the action progresses.

the pain of things

IN MEDIAS RES

J. L. CAMPBELL

The Pain of Things by J.L. Campbell

The Writers' Suite

Kingston, Jamaica

ISBN: 978-976-8307-51-4 (eBook edition)

ISBN: 978-976-8307-50-7 (Paperback edition)

one

SHANICE JACKSON WAS in danger and didn't know it. She was my target and the reason for my trip to Jamaica.

The man glaring at me blocked my view of the teenager. His gang of friends—a collection of three males wearing jeans, T-shirts, hoodies, and grillwork on their teeth—hovered, as if waiting for the opportune moment to pounce. They stepped in close, scowling, intent on keeping me from getting to Shanice.

Then, a barrage of gunfire erupted. The streetlights gave way in a shard of plastic that showered the sidewalk. The young hoodlums scattered in the darkness. Around me, the sound boxes continued blasting music with lewd lyrics.

I raced toward Shanice, who stood with both hands pressed to the sides of her head, and snagged her by the arm.

A bullet whizzed past my ear, leaving a trail of heat. My hand came away without any trace of blood, but it was still too close for comfort. "Get down!"

Shanice and I crouched beside a RAV4 parked next to the sidewalk. After a few tense seconds, I decided it was safe to move. The crush of bodies, as women screamed and ran in different directions, forced me to move fast. The darkness provided the necessary cover to help us escape and the dim glow coming from down the street provided all the light we needed.

Not for the first time, I wondered how the people around me could stand the noise and whether the sixteen-year-old girl at my side was in her right mind. She'd been giving me attitude from the moment I identified her from the close-up her parents had provided. Shanice was chock-full of resentment, but I didn't care. My business was to finish the job her parents had paid me generously to do.

She pulled away, twisting her hand, but I held on tight, knowing she'd slip away if given a chance.

"You have no right!" she screeched behind me, competing with the sound system.

My grip was firm but not bone-crushing as I led her through the panicked crowd. "Your parents gave me the right."

Another burst of gunfire had me sprinting toward the end of the street, where I'd parked the silver Hiace I rented when I landed on the island yesterday. A solid force collided with my chest and I stumbled but refused to release Shanice's hand. Shifting sideways, I dislodged the blubbering woman who streaked away as we moved against the crowd.

When we stopped, Shanice shivered in the early morning air. Her wide eyes gave away her fear, despite the bravado she wore like a shield. So much for the wannabe thug she'd been with. He'd left without a thought for her safety.

I yanked the car door open and touched her bare shoulder. "Get in."

She hesitated, then obeyed and shut the door.

At a trot, I went around to the other side, pulling off my windbreaker. When I sat next to her, I dropped it in her lap. "Put this on."

Eyes narrowed, she peered at me as if thinking about defying my order.

The blast from the air conditioner's vent hit Shanice and she shrugged on the jacket. She stared through the windscreen as if caught in her own world.

I figured she was probably thinking up lies to tell her distraught parents.

People moved back and forth in the road like a disturbed ant colony, and the reggae pounding in a steady thump added to the confusion. In the distance, blue lights flashed.

Since getting caught in a police dragnet wasn't part of my plan, I maneuvered out of the spot where I'd parked the car and threw a baleful glare at a man lurking close by with a knife in his hand. He looked like he was thinking about doing some damage.

Laying my hand on the horn, I reversed down the street bordered on each side by dilapidated zinc fences. In a flash, the car hit the Spanish Town Road, and we headed for New Kingston and the hotel where Shanice's parents waited.

She turned her head away from me as if fascinated by the sight of run-down buildings and people hanging out at street corner bars in the dead of night. Kingston was a city that never slept, according to Corinne, the woman I'd been seeing for a while now.

My gaze shifted to Shanice, who continued acting as if she was alone in the car.

I understood the classic signs of someone in defense mode. She didn't want anything to do with me and didn't plan to give an inch. We continued eastward in silence, with the hum of the engine and the air conditioner the only noise between us.

When we turned northward, she asked, "How do I know my parents sent you and that you won't rape me and dump me in a gully somewhere?"

Her abrupt words surprised me, along with how late the inquiry came. That should have been her first question, and it told me how innocent she was to the ways of the world, despite her act.

I glanced sideways at her. "Perhaps you should have thought of that before you skipped out on them."

She huffed, pulling the jacket tighter around her slim body. "That's not an answer."

Throwing her another look, I said, "It's the only one you're getting. Think about all the reasons it was downright stupid to disappear in a strange place with people you barely know."

As far as her parents and I understood the sequence of events, she'd been keeping company with a young man from Jamaica who she met in school in the States. Before she arrived on the island, she contacted him to let him know she was coming. He promised to show her the insider sights and sounds of the city along with his "crew," picked her up at the hotel, and went back to wherever he was staying.

"That's none of your business," she snapped, turning up her snub nose and whipping her head toward the window. From what I gathered, her parents had flown from the U.S. to Kingston on business. With Shanice on Easter break, they brought her with them. She told them she wanted to go to an event and they decided against it. Yesterday, while they were out at a seminar, she disappeared.

Through someone I'd previously worked for, the Jacksons accessed my number and flew me to the island from London, England, where I lived—when time allowed—and ran a distribution company. One crack at Shanice's laptop and I was able to tell them she'd left a decent trail on the Facebook messenger app.

With the assistance of a tech-savvy associate and his genius locator gadget that was connected to Google Maps, it was easy to follow Shanice's path into the inner city. Maxfield Avenue was a tough area, but Shanice had survived being holed up with her "friends." Only God knew what she'd done in that time, and it wasn't my business to ask. Suffice it to say, when I first spotted her she'd been simulating the sex act with one of the guys, or "daggering" as Jamaicans called it.

What she didn't know was that her "friends" had sent a note to her parents to demand money for her safe return. The Jacksons had been very clear that they didn't want even a whisper to reach the airwaves that their daughter had disappeared.

I didn't doubt Shanice may have ended up in harm's way if I hadn't found her in time. If the rescue went awry, or her parents hadn't been able to pay, they might have had to return to the States without her. The irony was, the girl had no idea that she was in a hostage situation.

Times like these made me grateful I didn't have children. More to the point, teenage daughters. My brother's kids brought enough drama and reminded me how blessed I was to be single. Because of what had happened in my first marriage, I'd had no intention of marrying again and kept to that decision for twenty years. Until Corinne.

Corinne Walker had me rethinking my current path. She knew nothing about this aspect of my life. As far as she was concerned, I roamed the well-known parts of Europe and the souks or market-places of Dubai, trading in coffee and spices while simultaneously earning easy money from my brother's investment skills.

She and my mother lived in blissful ignorance about the places I'd been and what I'd done in those locales. Both would have either a stroke or heart attack if they knew half of the dangers I faced.

We pulled up to the hotel property and my attention went to the barrier rail and the security guard, who tapped the window. When I lowered it, he asked my name and who I was there to visit.

Out of habit, I gave him an alias and both of us looked at Shanice when she let out a dramatic sigh.

"Are you okay, miss?" the security guard asked.

For a second, I thought she'd scream bloody murder. The warning glint in my eye must have transmitted accurately to her because she folded her arms and huffed like the spoilt child she was. In a nasty tone, she said, "I'm just fine."

The middle-aged man gave me a sympathetic smile and murmured. "The teen years are the worst."

My lips lifted in a pseudo-smile and I thanked him. He'd likely assumed I was a father trying to cope with his capricious daughter. As soon as we found a parking spot, Shanice attempted to get out of the vehicle.

"Not so fast," I said, detaining her with a hand on her shoulder.

If looks could kill, Shanice would have succeeded at running me through with a glare.

Her antics were lost on me. This was child's play compared to some of the extractions I'd done in the past. But I was thankful she seemed unmolested after being with thugs who ate girls like her for breakfast. What puzzled me, was that in a city of filled with upstanding citizens and a social set that would be more her speed, Shanice chose to embrace the company of men who belonged to the underbelly of society.

Meeting her gaze, I said, "You might think you're grown and all that, but you have a way to go yet."

Her mouth opened, and my raised hand stopped her from speaking.

"I don't believe you're the rotten, selfish little clot you've proven yourself to be through what you've done to your parents."

Shanice's eyes blazed, but again my restraining gesture stopped her words.

"I choose to believe you're better than what you've shown me tonight and I hope you think about redeeming yourself with your mom and dad." I kept the distaste out of my voice as I continued, "I don't plan to tell your parents what I found you doing, if you don't."

She had the grace to lower her gaze and bite her lip.

Good. "Are we clear?"

A tense couple of seconds slipped by before she nodded.

"We're done here."

We stepped out of the car and I stretched the kink out of my back and neck. The burning in my ear had eased, but it was a stark reminder that the evening could have ended differently. Corinne's mischievous grin and the burgundy locs she'd been sporting appeared in vivid color before my mind's eye. We were due to meet up at my nephew's christening next week. Spending time with her reminded me of being on assignment—anything could jump off where this facetious, independent seductress was concerned. For a forty-something woman, she was like a sprite—energetic and playful—which made for interesting times when we were alone.

I steered Shanice into the building and resolved to touch base with Corinne tonight. If luck was on my side, fate wouldn't have any other adventures lined up for me today.

two

ROGER CUT his eyes toward me and raised his voice. The clamor of the waves over the seashore competed with his accusation. "Corinne, you and I know you're lying."

In the last few minutes, we'd been talking about the length of time since we last saw each other. Roger was never shy to say how much he missed me when we weren't together. Me, not so much. I'd just been trying to convince him that I'd been too busy taking self-defense classes, staying fit, and planning my vacation, to miss him.

"Be that as it may." I shot Roger a disdainful look and continued walking. "I think we should close this conversation."

His sexy grin emerged as he kissed the corner of my mouth. "What the heck did you just say?"

His words annoyed me because they hit too close to home. I wanted to pull my hand out of his warm grip but refused to act on my feelings. Instead, I glanced sideways at him as we made our way along the beautiful beach in Antigua where my best friend, Khalila, and her husband, Douglas, were celebrating their son's christening.

"Never mind that. This is not the time to be indulging in heavy conversation. We're celebrating Zane and each other's company. Let's enjoy that."

“We still have to talk about us.” Although his tone was gentle, I didn’t miss the chiding note.

“But we don’t have to do it now.” Although I had the sense of being squeezed into a corner I wouldn’t be able to emerge from, I kept my tone light. “I don’t want to tell you any lies, especially when we just got out of church. Let me relish this celebration of my god-baby. Please.”

His lips twisted, then he said, “Fine. We’ll talk later.”

My nod was confident as I added, “Sure.”

For now, I had a reprieve, but no doubt Roger would circle back to the subject of our relationship the first chance he got.

We climbed the back steps of his mother’s guest house, a two-story building surrounded by a carpet of grass and fruit trees, including Otaheite apples, mangoes, papaya and soursop. Since our arrival, Roger and I gorged ourselves on the miniature “apple” bananas that grew in one corner of the property. That wasn’t the only thing we’d done in the grass under the tree, while acting as if we were teenagers with hormones running wild.

Hyacinth Blythe catered to return vacationers, who were like family to her. My favorite part of the property was the beach, accessible from the back of the house. The picturesque view and rustic furniture close to the shoreline were part of the charm of the property. I’d visited after the New Year, when Khalila flew in for a week to plan the christening. Miss Hyacinth and I had renewed our acquaintance then.

At that time, I found out she was aware that Roger and I were an item. So much for thinking we’d been discreet around her when we met at Khalila’s wedding and again after Zane’s birth last September. Both times, we’d barely been able to be in the same room without falling into each other’s arms.

The fact that Roger and I lived in different places kept our relationship fresh. He texted or sent WhatsApp messages when he was out of range, which made me appreciate him even more. Now that we were together, my nerve endings kept me in a perpetual state of expectancy. But we had to get through this evening before he could satisfy me with his loving again.

I went to the ladies' room and took care of my needs while my thoughts refused to leave the man outside.

Roger was leaning in the passage when I came out of the bathroom.

I laid both hands on his chest and reveled in the firm flesh beneath my palms. Roger was muscular and energetic for someone who claimed he didn't get enough physical activity. The soft fabric of his baby-blue silk shirt complemented the navy jacket he'd cast aside the moment we walked out of the church. He was freshly shaved and his hair was cut close to the scalp, which made him look exactly like his older brother. The only difference between them was that Roger wasn't as thick as Doug. They were both tall, dark-skinned, and distinguished.

The two brothers were also good-natured and self-possessed. Not much moved them to excitement, except the sport of golf. They traveled to various countries to play in tournaments and watched all the Majors on television. Aside from that, they both bought expensive golfing equipment and took lessons to keep their game sharp.

Despite their similarities, Roger stood out to me. I still remembered the first time we met over dinner with Doug and Khalila. The strong handshake, the sparkle in his eyes, and the friendly smile had intrigued me and made me feel something I hadn't in a while—unabashed interest. I'd had lovers in the past, but ever since I parted with the one who broke my heart a dozen years ago, I prided myself on my independence and always being in control of my emotions. I used men to pass the time until the next one piqued my interest.

They were often much younger than I, which suited me. These men weren't looking for responsibility and I wasn't looking for love. Roger was only two years my junior, but my interest in him went deeper than the surface, which excited and worried me. Because that indicated I was falling for him, which meant bye-bye to my freedom to do as I liked, as well as emotional control.

Roger ran his fingers back and forth on my bare skin. His fingertips were slightly rough, but I enjoyed his touch. The white linen sleeveless dress I wore gave him easy access, and he lowered his head to kiss my shoulder. My skin tingled where his lips made contact and brought back memories of our passionate night together.

My lips brushed his chin and I murmured, “Let’s head back outside.”

“You’re afraid of me now?” he chuckled and backed me against the wall, imprisoning me with his hands on both sides of my head.

“Not at all, I just don’t want anybody to think we snuck away like a couple of horny teenagers.”

Roger laughed. “If I didn’t know better, I’d say you were spending too much time with Mama. That’s just the sort of thing she’d say.”

I wriggled against him, knowing the effect it would have on him. “So, lemme go then.”

He spoke next to my ear in a husky, low tone. “Not before I steal a few more kisses from you. With all these people around, who knows when I’ll get another chance.”

My arms slid around his neck, and he pressed in close and treated me to a deep kiss. His tongue surged into my mouth and tangled with mine as if we had all day to explore each other. One of his thighs slid between mine and my core tingled with need. By the time he raised his head, I wanted to forget about the social side of Zane’s christening and find a more private space.

Roger had been gung-ho about us spending most of our time together when we both arrived in Antigua. Since Douglas introduced us, I’d been happy to meet Roger in various hotels in Montego Bay and Miami.

Our romantic encounters in the last eighteen months had been exhilarating and reminded me of all I’d denied myself by flitting from one man to another. I also loved the adventure and excitement of those sudden getaways, based on Roger’s erratic schedule. He promised me a trip to London, but our schedules hadn't allowed for the visit as yet.

My relationship with Roger was ideal. After what I'd been through, I preferred to keep my interaction with men at a particular level. Now Roger was demanding more.

During all this time, we'd been content to enjoy each other's company and meet up every couple of months when Roger's business took him to Miami. Jamaica was a hop and a skip away, and when he came to the island, those interludes satisfied my libido and the need for companionship. What changed since the last time we met, I didn't know, but I'd find out.

I didn't want to be in a position where one day the person who meant the most might walk away if something happened that he couldn't handle. I'd been through that once and it nearly broke me. At this point in my life, I couldn't walk that road again.

Roger was easy to communicate with, and a good listener, which made for some awkward conversations when I intended to keep my connection with him at a casual level. The man could pull emotions out of me I didn't even know I was carrying. Like the time I almost told him the true reason I'd become an exercise buff had more to do with keeping my body and mind occupied than the need for physical fitness.

From inside the kitchen, the voice of Miss Hyacinth, his mother, interrupted our interlude. "You two better stop acting like you're sixteen-year-old kids and join di rest of us outside."

"That's not what we're doing, Mama," Roger called out, without looking away from me.

She chuckled and poked her head through the doorway. Her eyes danced in her cheerful face. "Try telling dat to someone else. Di two of yuh barely have eyes for anybody else. If I leave yuh alone, yuh won' be saving anyt'ing for later."

Roger and I looked at each other and burst out laughing.

* * *

Doug and Khalila made a wonderful couple, and Zane was a heart-snatching addition to the family. At six months, he was bright-eyed, chubby, and good-natured. He was also friendly, which meant he'd been handed around the gathering with his sharp-eyed grandmother keeping watch and approving who held him. Now, it was my turn and Zane gave me a smile that melted my heart. He now had four teeth which were on full display as he grinned at me.

"You're all kinds of special, but you know that, Master Blythe."

He gurgled, as if he understood every word. I'd never been particularly crazy about babies, but after Khalila got me involved in naming Zane, I started stalking Instagram and looking at pictures of cute infants and toddlers.

With Zane in my arms, I scanned the huge tent Doug had rented for the reception. Neither he nor his brother was in sight. They were probably holed up somewhere discussing money. I wandered toward the sea, which was a lifelong source of fascination for me.

My work in human resources ate a major chunk of each day and cleaning up at home on the weekends, plus taking care of errands, didn't leave me a lot of time for trips to the beach, a half-hour away. The pleasant breeze and the shade trees combated the effect of the brilliant sun. The Blythe family's friends and relatives sat under the tent chatting and laughing as if they had no worries.

I shifted Zane to my other hip. His bottom felt squishy, so I headed toward the house to change him. The guesthouse occupied two floors and Zane's small utility box with baby wipes, diapers, and diaper rash cream were on the bottom level in the room where I slept. The bedroom was cool, but I turned on the overhead fan and laid Zane on the bed. Walking backward, I pointed at him. "Don't move."

He smiled wide, but stayed where I laid him.

I grabbed the bag with his diapers and wipes and prepared to change him. The job was half done, and I was still whispering nonsense to Zane when Doug's voice floated in through the window. "So, Rodge, how was Jamaica?"

I frowned. He'd been in Jamaica? When? My hands stilled as I waited for Roger's response.

He released a lengthy chuckle. "I wasn't there long enough to enjoy anything. I was in and out once I located that girl."

"Another one sealed away," Doug said with a proud note in his voice.

"Yep. Everybody happy and all that."

Mystified, I eased Zane's tiny white pants up to his waist and smoothed the matching satin shirt over his tummy.

A momentary pause dropped into the conversation before Doug cleared his throat. "Have you given any thought to—"

"Don't start that again," Roger said. "Please."

"Fine. I'll leave it alone for now. I just don't want it to come as an unpleasant surprise one day when Mama hears that you were sh—"

"It won't happen. Keep the faith."

"Trust me, little brother, I pray for you more often than I pray for myself."

My face crumpled into an intense frown. What on earth was Roger involved in that needed that kind of intervention from Doug? The more I thought about it, the more I hoped they weren't involved in anything illegal. But no, not if I went by his earlier words about finding a girl. And what did that mean?

I was annoyed that he'd been on the island and hadn't said a peep about his trip. What was there to hide if he was in Jamaica on legitimate business? Resentment settled over me and I thought about how to get more information out of Roger. What reason did he have to hide anything from me? I'd never acted possessive, but with men one never knew. I'd found out first-hand how deceptive and shallow they could be.

Zane let out a squeal, which brought my mind back to what I was supposed to be doing. My gaze shot to the window. With the wind factor, it was unlikely they'd heard Zane. I wiped his face and hands and dropped a kiss on his forehead. Then, we returned to the cluster of family and friends gathered in the back yard.

As I descended the steps, Roger walked away from Doug. "Where've you been?"

I pointed over my shoulder. "Duty called with your nephew."

He took him from my arms, making much of him and acting outraged when Zane grabbed his cheeks.

I was dying to bring up his trip to Jamaica but didn't want it to be obvious I'd been eavesdropping.

He looked at me while Zane released a series of happy yelps. "You all right?"

While holding down my dress, which the wind threatened to yank from me, I forced a smile. "Why wouldn't I be?"

"Answering a question with a question isn't a good sign." His eyes searched mine as if he'd missed something. Then Zane pulled his attention away by grabbing his collar.

Since he gave me the opening I needed, I used it. Eyebrows raised, I asked, "Did you do something you need to be worried about?"

Roger's gaze flickered and he angled his head toward me, locking his eyes with mine. "Are you accusing me of something, Corinne?"

In a casual tone, I said, "Nothing at all."

Inside, I was all kinds of twisted up. I'd been too obvious, and if I asked him anything about where he'd been, Roger would know I'd been in earshot of him and his brother.

"Corinne," Miss Hyacinth called from where she sat under the tent. "Bring my grandbaby over here, please."

Eager to escape Roger's intense study, I took Zane from him and walked the few feet across the sand to where his mother was holding court. Miss Hyacinth presided over a table decorated with blue and white balloon toppers with Zane's name imprinted on them. She invited me to stay and introduced me to a gaggle of her church sisters. The opposite of her sons in terms of height, Miss Hyacinth was stout with a commanding presence. She'd adopted me into the family, along with Khalila, and wielded her authority whenever she thought it necessary.

At the other side of the tent, Doug's daughters, Monique and Kimone, hunched over their phones among a set of young adults. The two girls would be twenty and eighteen this year, and had adjusted to Doug and Khalila's marriage after some rough patches, including the loss of their mother. Mo grinned and looked up from her phone. When our eyes met, she waved.

After greeting her, I accepted a glass of pink lemonade from a waiter, which I sipped. The concoction of cranberry juice, lemon juice, and granulated sugar carried just the right level of tartness. When I placed the glass on the table, my attention strayed to where I left Roger.

He wasn't there, but a few feet to the right under a palm tree. Doug and he were deep in conversation. They stood side by side with both hands shoved into their pants pockets.

Before I looked away, I realized they were talking about me. Or so I assumed, since both of them stared at me with concern etched on their faces.

three

"I'LL GET THERE tomorrow afternoon. When I land I'll be in touch."

The idyllic vacation I planned to spend with Corinne zipped out the window. I dropped the phone in my lap and closed my eyes, formulating what I needed to say to the woman who I'd had the devil of a time convincing to give me an entire week of her life.

I'd grown restless and discontented each time Corinne and I met for a few days here and there, then went about our individual business. It was never my intention to settle with her, but she'd taken me unawares. I missed her when we weren't together.

One night, after a bloody run-in with a group of guerrillas in Colombia, I wondered how she'd deal with hearing that I hadn't survived, if the outcome was different. Would she miss me? How would she feel knowing she hadn't been able to say goodbye? Only sheer force of will prevented me from calling her in the middle of the night.

The next morning, I barely waited for the crack of dawn to ring her number and couldn't believe how much I wanted to tell her that I needed us to be together all the time. But my life wasn't structured to accommodate a life partner. My movements made it difficult to predict where I'd be at any given time, and Corinne wasn't the type to wait patiently at home while I completed assignments in various countries. All of this rationalizing left me in limbo, and that wasn't where I wanted to be with Corinne.

The breeze coming off the waves was soothing and reminded me how her touch had the power to center me. Like the familiarity of the cooling wind I missed when I wasn't at home, Corinne made my quality of life better simply by being at my side.

This, right here, was heavenly. The shade from the palm trees provided cover from the sun and kept the back yard cool. The only discordant note was Doug, who'd been asking questions I'd been avoiding for the last couple of days.

He sipped from the beer bottle, then placed it on the wooden table between us. The sturdy beach chairs our father had made by hand in his spare time creaked under Doug's weight as he settled his feet in the sand. "So, you're taking on another job, huh?"

"It's what I do for a living," I said, without opening my eyes.

Doug's voice intruded on the peace I was trying to find. "When d'you plan to tell Corinne how you make your money? At least, some of it?"

I stared into eyes the same shade of brown as mine. People said we resembled each other closely enough to be twins. His bald head, thick moustache, above-average height, and authoritative presence made people think Doug was a security expert, but aside from a stint in the local army, he wasn't interested in anything along those lines.

What he excelled at was making money, and he'd earned plenty of it for me over the years. If I wanted to, I could retire comfortably, but our mother had instilled a strong work ethic in our blood. So had our deceased father.

"Do you intend to tell her at all?" Doug asked.

"Why would you ask that?" Resentment reared its head. We'd had this conversation several times already since Saturday. At some point, I'd have to do what he was urging, but Corinne would have issues. I was sure of it. My challenge was that I didn't know how to handle the concerns she'd have and the difficult questions she'd ask.

"Well, you've been seeing each other on and off for a couple of years now and—"

"Almost nineteen months. I don't need you to tell me how long we've been together."

Doug's elevated eyebrows mocked me. "So, you admit you have something going on?"

My nostrils flared. "Don't be an asshole."

He shrugged, unperturbed. "All I'm saying is, if you intend to get serious about Corinne, you should tell her you do more than peddle spices and coffee."

With my focus on the tranquil blue-green waves, I answered, "I'll tell her soon."

When I looked at him, one side of Doug's mouth curled. "Some time before Zane attains manhood, I hope."

"Mind your business."

Raising one shoulder in a shrug, Doug said, "Hey, you know me. I'm only asking because she's my wife's bestie and if you hurt her in any way, Khalila's gonna come for me. You don't want to be around that woman when she's upset about something."

My laughter was long and loud. "Don't tell me Khalila has you whipped."

Doug sipped from his beer again, then relaxed against the canvas straps on the back of the seat. "Call it what you will. *You* don't have a wife and don't have to live with mine."

"Are you saying she's miserable?" That took me by surprise because Doug and Khalila seemed to have found paradise with each other. My brother laughed easily and was more relaxed since Khalila entered his life.

Doug gave me an evil look. "Not at all. But if my wife is happy, I'm happy. If my wife is disturbed, my life becomes hellish. If *you're* involved in making that happen, *I'm* going to come for you."

I laughed again. "I'm sure you know Corinne can take care of herself."

"Agreed." He stared at me, tipping his head sideways. "But the two of you have a soft spot for each other. You'd better do something about it before some man who's ready and can handle that much woman comes along and snatches her away while you're globe-trotting being a fixer."

"Good food for thought, bro." I nodded, although still unwilling to commit to telling Corinne about the extractions. What would I stay to her? Only God knew how she'd react to me putting my life in danger during the times we were apart. She didn't try to control me, but she'd have a thing or two to say about me keeping secrets.

Each time we were together, I wanted more of Corinne. So far, I hadn't done much about it other than ask for all of her time while she was here.

"Plus Mama likes her. That's good. You have half the battle won."

"This marriage thing really has turned your head." I studied him, as if that would give me more insight into the person he'd become since he re-married. "Used to be, you wouldn't give a rat's ass if Mama liked who you were seeing, now..."

"You have to admit, it makes life a lot easier. No man wants to be between his wife and a mother-in-law who hates her."

"That's true. Rosalie's mother was hard to deal with, and we were only married for three years."

As the waves crashed against the shore a feet away, Doug squinted at me. "Mmmm. You haven't mentioned her in years."

"Why would I?" After a few seconds, I still felt him staring at me. "It's not as painful as it was anymore. I've made peace with it, I think."

"That's good to know."

I'd gotten married when I was twenty-four and my wife was pregnant within a couple of years. At that time I worked as an insurance agent. While I was on the other side of the island, Rosalie had gone into early labor. By the time I got to the hospital, she'd been hemorrhaging and when I saw her, she was as pale as if all the life-giving liquid had drained out of her. She died hours later. Our son didn't survive.

For months, I lived in a vacuum, and when I recovered from the pain of the double loss, my job turned into medicine. I didn't have to think, and making sales kept me occupied. The company also benefitted from having me as the top sales agent for six consecutive quarters. The years passed and I overcame my loneliness with work and helping other people find their loved ones. A few relationships happened here and there, but I didn't allow myself to get attached.

Until Corinne.

"When d'you have to leave?" Doug asked after a sip of beer.

"Tonight."

His gaze met mine and he cocked one brow. "What are you gonna tell her?"

"I have urgent business." Coming off my lips, the words already sounded inadequate.

"There's no better time than the present." He stared past me, tipping his chin. "Here she comes now."

I followed the path of his gaze to where Corinne approached with Zane in her arms. The cream dress hid her firm calves and toned legs, the strength of which impressed me every time she wrapped them around me. She kept a careful eye on the sand while Zane played with her locs. When she stood next to Doug, she settled the baby in his lap. "Live delivery from Mommy Dearest."

Doug chuckled and lifted his son to stand on his legs. "A bit too much for her to handle, huh?"

Zane bobbed on his father's thighs and squealed his delight.

"He is, when she's trying to make that potato salad you like so much."

Taking Corinne by the hand, I got to my feet. "Walk with me."

Doug gave me an approving wink over Zane's head.

I linked my fingers with Corinne's and pointed out to sea. "The beach and all that open space makes me think of how limitless life is, the wonderful possibilities."

Nodding in agreement, Corinne said, "I understand. It's that kind of thinking that made me decide to take so much time off from the office. Lately, I've been wanting a change."

Corinne worked in human resources at an investment bank, and I always thought she enjoyed her job, so this was new information. Noting the introspective tone of her voice, I studied her profile. "So, what are you going to do with all of those one hundred and eighty days?"

Corinne tipped her head back and gave me her usual mischievous smile. "I haven't planned every minute of my holiday. I'm doing that a little at a time. Doing whatever I feel like doing, when I feel like doing it. I have some stuff on my bucket list."

"Anything exciting?" I squeezed her fingers between mine. I missed her already, but duty called.

She gave me a side-eye and nodded. "Wouldn't you like to know."

"Of course, I would. I hoped you were planning to spend a significant portion of that time with me."

She stopped and looked up at me with a mysterious smile in place. "Seriously?"

"Why would you doubt that I'd want to be with you? I almost had to grovel to get you to come here."

Corinne slapped my arm. "That's not quite how it went."

I dragged a hand over the back of my neck. "That's exactly what it felt like, and this would have been the first time we spent an entire week together."

"True. It's always been three to five days here and there."

"We seriously need to change that, especially since you don't have to be anywhere in particular." For some reason, I hesitated to tell her that I was leaving, but put aside my reluctance and brought her fingers to my lips and kissed them. "We'll rectify that after I come back."

Corinne shot me a suspicious look. "You're leaving when?"

"Later this evening."

"And you've known this for how long?" she asked, her tone cool.

"Fifteen minutes." I tensed, waiting for her reaction.

"Oh. Wow." Corinne's tone was thoughtful, rather than surprised. We walked a few more paces before she asked, "When d'you return?"

"Hopefully, in a couple of days."

"Who knew coffee and spices could be this urgent." She wore a pseudo-innocent expression, as if giving me space to deny her assertion.

When I didn't speak, she tried to ease her hand out of mine but I wouldn't let go because I needed to savor every moment of contact before I had to board that plane. "Enjoy the time you have left on the island. Get Mama to tell you about all the places the tourists don't get to visit. When I'm back, I'll take you on a personal tour."

Corinne eyed me as if she didn't think I'd return. "We'll see."

"You don't believe me?"

"Like I said, time will tell." All traces of patience left her face. "When exactly are you coming back from this coffee jaunt anyway?"

Since I couldn't give a direct answer, depending on what situation I found when I got to Brasilia, I hedged. "Should be a few days."

"You know I won't be twiddling my thumbs waiting for you to come back?"

"I'd never be selfish enough to ask you to do that if I didn't think I'd be returning soon."

"I've never thought of you as selfish, but if I think you're wasting my time, I'll move along *without* you."

I stopped her by tugging on her fingers. "If you leave, I *will* come to Jamaica and find you."

She gave me a sweet smile that was more of a challenge than anything else. "Who says I'll be in Jamaica?"

"Don't give me a hard time, woman," I said, putting extra bass in my voice to let her know how serious I was.

Corinne arched her eyebrows and pulled her hand out of mine. "Trust me, I'm not. You do what you have to do and I'll do what pleases me."

Her casual attitude unsettled me. She was acting as if I'd deliberately sabotaged our plans. I would have preferred to stay with her, but I made a commitment I had to honor. If Corinne didn't believe I'd keep my word, I had to find a way to convince her. At the back of my mind was the thought that I'd also have to keep my fingers crossed that no jobs would pop up and prevent me from coming back, or disrupt our time together after I returned.

four

KHALILA CHOSE a great place for lunch. The seafood restaurant overlooked the water and the rustic furnishings and laid-back atmosphere added to our relaxation. The eager waiter finally left us when we told him we were happy with his service and our meals.

Miss Hyacinth and Doug opted to stay at the guesthouse when we decided to go shopping downtown. We didn't mind, since it gave us time to talk alone. While Khalila ate, I kept Zane busy. Now it was her turn to watch me eat.

Over the table, her eyes sparkled. "That sounds exciting. I wish I could come with you."

I sucked my teeth. "Right. You're exactly where you want to be. I'd love to see you taking off for parts unknown with Doug's baby in tow."

She laughed, then looked out to sea and back at me. "You're right. He'd have a fit."

That started me laughing. "For a man who didn't want a baby, he's certainly relishing his role."

A dreamy smile took over Khalila's face as she removed a lock of her hair from Zane's mouth. Her honey-brown skin was sun-kissed after all the running around she did last weekend on the beach to prepare for Zane's christening. She'd put on a little weight since having Zane, but in comparison to her generous curves, I looked like the cartoon character, Olive Oyl, but with bumps and dips in the right places. We'd laughed about it this morning when we looked at ourselves side by side in jeans and tee-shirts before we left the cottage. I'd moved in and stayed with them since Khalila's parents left.

"You can say that again," Khalila gushed. "And he's efficient at it. Feeding, changing diapers, you name it, Doug's got it down to a fine art."

"Be thankful he's a good husband and dad."

She nodded, then sighed. "Yes, my life has turned out so much better than I imagined."

The shadows in her eyes told me her mind had wandered to earlier days when she'd fallen into the pit of depression. I patted her hand to bring her back to our conversation. "The two of you are great together. You should have met years ago."

"I'm not so sure about that." She stroked Zane's head with gentle finger. "If we had, then I wouldn't have given birth to Amir."

The mention of her son, who'd been killed in an accident during his teen years, was a sobering thought, which brought my own tragedy to mind.

"That's true," I admitted, as more memories surfaced.

My baby girl hadn't made it past a traumatic premature birth. Even now, the thought of it brought such sadness I wanted to push the memory to the back of my mind. But I hadn't dealt with the loss as I should have. Instead of examining all the issues surrounding Nadia's death and dealing with them, I pushed them into the deepest part of my subconscious. So, after more than a decade—twelve years, to be exact—I still had issues.

Only my love for Khalila, and living vicariously through her, kept me from looking too deeply at the nothingness my life had been for a while now. Work. The current man. More work. I broke the monotony by putting my body through a rigorous exercise routine at the gym each week.

Roger had made something of a difference. For starters, he was closer to my age than the other men I'd seen over the years. At forty-one to my forty-three, he was still more mature than anyone I'd been with up to this point. Yet, now that he was interested in having more than casual sex, I was hesitant about committing to anything deeper.

Khalila touched my hand. "Don't go there, Corinne."

Her warning had come a little too late, but I smiled. "I'm fine."

"Are you sure?" she asked, peering into my eyes.

"Yes, I'm good." When the concern didn't fade from her gaze, I added, "For real."

She watched me for a few more minutes as I finished my lunch of curried shrimp, rice, and steamed vegetables, and shifted Zane to her other leg. "What's next on your looooong vacation?"

"Roger tells me he's coming back in the next couple of days, so I'll stick around and enjoy some time with him. Then I may fly to Miami to visit family. Good thing we're coming out of the Easter season. Otherwise, the fares would be astronomical."

"True." Khalila fed Zane a tiny bit of cherry from her glass of limeade.

He made a sour face then smiled when the sweetness kicked in.

"You know," Khalila said, sitting forward, "Roger isn't—how should I say this?—reliable when it comes to being in any place when he says he will be."

"I'd be blind if I didn't catch on to that by now, Lila."

We both laughed because Roger had a reputation of being early for nothing. He simply showed up—on time, if the occasion was important, sometimes late, or not at all. Yet, he didn't give the impression of being irresponsible. He usually stayed in touch with me and chalked up his absence to business demands. Always.

"I know." Khalila opened Zane's fist to release her hair, then added, "It's just that I don't want him to disappoint you."

"Trust me, I understand." I poked the last shrimp with my fork and chuckled when I finished chewing. "You know perfectly well that I can take care of myself. If Roger doesn't come back, I'll move on without him."

"The finality in that tells me you'll get it into your head to ditch him."

Other than an evil grin, all I said was, "You know me so well."

"Okay. So aside from the Miami stopover, what else is on your list?"

I laid the napkin aside, sipped from my water glass, then pushed it away. "Remember those self-defense classes I wanted to take?"

Khalila nodded and captured some of her hair behind one ear.

"Well, I completed that."

She put up a hand and we shared a high-five, grinning like thieves in cahoots.

Zane raised his hand and I gave him one, too.

"Working with ceramic is clearly not my speed, so I think sky-diving or jet-skiing may be next. I also want to take one of those adventure tours in Ocho Rios." I propped my chin on one hand. "A trip to the Bahamas and somewhere in South America is also on my list."

"Seriously? Without me?"

While laughing, I tickled Zane across the bistro table. "You know I've been wanting to do that for a long time."

"That's true." She sighed while stroking her son's cheek. "I'm green with envy, but you deserve it, so enjoy yourself."

I played with the straw in my mango coconut daiquiri, while deciding whether I should share my suspicions with Khalila. She'd never broken my confidence before, and we shared everything. After a sip, I said, "I think Roger is into something dangerous."

She pushed her plate farther away from Zane's grasping hands and repositioned him, frowning all the while. "What?"

"I heard him and Doug talking after the christening."

"I'm sure there's an explanation for whatever you heard."

"I'm sure there is, too," I said dryly. "Pity I can't ask, since I overheard them while changing Zane."

"He travels a fair bit, but Roger would never do anything—"

I shot her an incredulous look over the rim of my glass. "And how exactly would you know if he's doing anything fishy?"

"Well, for one, Doug wouldn't knowingly condone anything like that."

"And two?" I sat forward, waiting for what she'd say.

"You should give Roger the benefit of the doubt. Why not ask him if you want to know exactly what else you think he might be involved in?"

"It's not like I didn't try, but—"

She rolled her eyes. "If I know you, and I'm sure I do, you came at him sideways with a half accusation."

I opened my mouth, but couldn't voice the denial.

With a satisfied smile in place, Khalila said, "I knew it. Isn't it easier to just ask the man some direct questions?"

"Well, couldn't he be honest enough to tell me what else he's doing under the guise of selling coffee and spices? Or maybe, I should say what he's doing aside from that business."

"That's if he's doing any such thing."

I smirked, thinking back to Doug and Roger's conversation. "Trust me, Roger is doing something you don't know about."

"I'm sure he'll tell you when he's ready for you to know. Give him time."

An unpleasant thought blindsided me. "He'd better not be involved in any dodgy business that would ruin me by association."

While I didn't think of myself as higher or better than anyone else, my reputation and position as HR Director at the NLJ Investment Bank were important to me. The company was listed on the local stock exchange and was in the news often for the strides made in the last decade. I enjoyed my job, and though I hadn't lived the life of a saint, I also hadn't flaunted my short-lived relationships by being too much in the public eye.

My cell rang and when I dug it out of my bag, a lopsided smile claimed my lips. I held up the cellular. “Speak of the devil.”

Eyebrows raised, Khalila said, “Roger?”

I nodded while swiping the phone screen.

“Corinne, are you still in Antigua?”

“Where else would I be?” My smile grew wider and my heart rate accelerated as I sassed him.

Roger’s voice was crisp as if he was sitting next to me. “D’you remember telling me I’d better haul my tail back or else ...”

“Not in those words,” I said as warmth seeped through my body and settled in all the places Roger had touched a few days ago. This man had me feeling more excited than I’d been in years. For too long, I’d been having relationships that didn’t matter. Right now, I wished he was beside me instead of hundreds of miles away.

His smooth baritone interrupted my thoughts. “I’ll be back tomorrow afternoon and I’m taking you somewhere special in the evening. Wear something sexy and take a bathing suit.”

I let out a sigh and couldn’t hide my ear-to-ear grin. “That sounds wonderful.”

“I’m on the move, love. See you then.”

When I looked up, Khalila was grinning over Zane’s shoulder. “That was quick conversation.”

“Roger and Doug are brothers,” was all I said.

She burst out laughing. “Straight. No chaser, right?”

“Exactly.”

“From your expression, I know he’ll be here soon.”

“That’s right.” Delighted laughter poured out of me as I hugged myself. “Girl, I don’t know what he’s done to me, but I can’t wait to see him!”

five

CORINNE WAS STRAIGHT UP GOING to kill me. This time, the job took me to a depressed area in Port of Spain, Trinidad. The town was Laventille, and although it held the reputation for being the birthplace of steel pan music, there was also a crime problem. Good people resided in the densely populated town, but criminal elements had the community in a choke hold.

When I arrived in Trinidad and Tobago, a cab driver met me in front of the Piarco International Airport and deposited me at a hotel five minutes away. The room was decent and from the material in the desk drawer, I gathered that a mall and restaurant were within in a five-minute range. My man on the ground, Eddie McCrane, had not yet been in touch with me, but I expected him to contact me by phone. While I waited, I checked my messages and tried not to think about Corinne.

From the start, she'd been on my mind. In fact, she never left since we spoke two days ago when I was supposed to be headed back home. She occupied my thoughts on the flight, to the point where I wondered if I could keep my mind on the current assignment. Yesterday, I'd been booked on a flight from Brasilia to Antigua. Hours before my flight, I took a phone call which resulted in me cancelling my flight and re-routing to Port of Spain.

My next telephone conversation after that was with Corinne. When I told her I'd likely be delayed for another two days at least, she went silent.

"Babe, I'll make it up to you."

"I don't need empty promises, so save it."

She then gave me an earful, while I stared out the window at the metropolis below.

"If I'm not high enough on your agenda for you to come back like you promised, then I can only see this relationship going downhill from here."

I gave her the excuse of extended meetings, but she wasn't buying that explanation.

After another barrage of words, Corinne quieted down. "Isn't it easier if you simply tell me the truth?" she asked. "Is there another woman involved? I'm not a weakling. If that's the situation, just be up front about it. I'd respect you so much more."

"That's not it. Corinne, I—"

"Roger, don't do this. It really doesn't matter. No need to make up any stories to pacify me."

I called her name again, but she was gone. If and when I chose to explain this part of my life, the phone wasn't the place to do it, but Corinne's response was no surprise. She was hot-headed and hot-blooded. Those facets of her character were already working against me. Before I did anything else, I sent her a text to apologize again and hoped she'd read it.

Eddie rang to confirm he'd pick me up in a half-hour and during that time, I did a mental review of my Skype telephone conference with Ralph Moray, the owner of the company whose worker had gone missing. Moray thought his most prolific sales representative had been taken hostage by gang members who needed ready access to pharmaceutical products. Since they had frequent run-ins with the local police, Moray thought they needed certain medication, which Duran Myers had refused to supply. In earlier correspondence with his boss, he hinted this was the case.

My contact, Eddie, was an American who'd gone to Trinidad on business, liked the lay of the land and married a local. Private investigation was his line of business, so he'd already put out feelers and received intel that Myers had been spotted in a cab with a couple other men, heading to Laventille two days ago.

He'd been taken on his way home from work the previous week and had been kept hidden since then. The new sighting had encouraged his employer to bring me in to help wrap up a dangerous situation. Eddie believed Myers's captors were moving him around to avoid detection until the two million U.S. dollar ransom they demanded was paid for his safe return.

"I'm glad Ralph got you here," Eddie said, when we shook hands in the lobby.

We stood at the same height and his golden-brown skin had the seared look of someone who spent too much time in the sun, but his friendly demeanor put me at ease.

With a sharp nod, he added, "A fresh pair of eyes may give us a different angle on the data we have."

"I hope I can help resolve this situation, but with kidnappings you never know."

Dragging one hand over his thick beard, Eddie motioned me toward the entrance. "And these guys here do not play. They've turned kidnapping into a thriving business and kill without remorse."

"I've heard, but let's meet with your informant and move from that point."

We walked to the plaza next door and sat in a busy café waiting for Eddie's informer to show.

"Here he comes now," Eddie murmured and tipped his head toward the plate glass door.

The moment I laid eyes on Bhavin Rice, the word *unreliable* slammed me in the gut. I also knew, without being told, that his name was an alias. The half-Indian man in tight jeans and a fake UVO tee-shirt walked tentatively, as if he expected to be accosted at any moment.

He slid into the seat across from me, smelling of weed. His close-set eyes scanned the half-empty café floor. We'd been careful to choose a table in a corner, so he had no reason to be this jumpy. Unless he thought someone had followed him. Even while Eddie introduced us, Bhavin didn't maintain eye contact and seemed nervous and high. Each time I moved, Bhavin twitched and seemed ready to sprint away from the table. He took several sips of the Carib beer we ordered, and I hoped it would take the edge off and calm him a little.

"So, Bhavin, tell us how you know where the man we're looking for is being held."

He jerked and grabbed the beer bottle tight, frowning at the label as if my directness was too much for him.

"Come on, Bhavin. Don't be shy now." Eddie glared at him. "We don't have time to waste."

"I tol' you I does know because I hear dem others talkin' about where deh keeping him."

I stayed quiet and listened hard to decipher the conversation between the two men. Bhavin's accent needed all my focus.

"So help me God, if you waste my time—" Eddie fisted one hand on the table, and Bhavin shrank against the seat.

"I see him wid my two eyes." Bhavin waggled one finger in front of his face to emphasize his point. "He had on a wedding band and carried one of them zip-up cases that does hold documents."

"You better be sure you had nothing to do with this." Eddie's bleak gaze confirmed that Bhavin's information was accurate.

"I'm not into dem things as you well know," Bhavin shot back.

"We'll see about that. Let's go."

"I will take you, but I have to make a stop and meet you in one hour." Bhavin emphasized the time by holding up one finger.

The look I gave Eddie across the table had him raising one hand.

We watched Bhavin walk away before Eddie got out his phone and typed a message. He raised his head a moment later and met my concerned gaze. "I have someone tailing him."

"Good, because I don't like surprises."

A faint smile lit Eddie's face. "Neither do I. We can't afford them in this business."

He ordered coconut water and lime for us, and when the waiter delivered the glasses and walked away, Eddie outlined the entire sequence of events leading up to and including the kidnapping.

"Myers has a family," Eddie concluded, "and I'd hate for Ralph Moray to have to tell his employee's wife that we didn't get him back alive."

"I'm with you on that. I'm thinking—"

Eddie's phone rang and he put up a finger to stop me. The longer he listened, the fiercer his frown grew, until he hissed and spat a swearword. When he hung up, he explained that Bhavin had met another man across town—a member of the gang Eddie suspected had kidnapped Myers.

"Knowing that little rat, he's planning to double-cross us." Eddie got to his feet. "Let's meet him halfway."

"I don't think that's best." I swallowed the last of my drink and motioned for him to sit. "You'll make him suspicious if you intercept him. Let him come back here. When we see what he's got, we'll make our move."

He thought about it, then nodded. "You're right. I know where he is and that's what's important, but we have some work to do, so let's go."

We walked down the avenue and around the corner to a two-story building, where Eddie did business. Eddie led me behind a reception-cum-office area crammed with filing cabinets and several cubicles occupied by employees hunched in front of computers.

I sat in his cramped office while he opened a huge metal safe in one corner of the room.

On the desk, he laid a Ruger .357 mag. While he loaded the

weapon, he said, "I know you're carrying, but we have to be careful here so I don't walk around with a gun all the time. The gangs have made the police crack down on everybody."

I didn't ask how he knew I was armed, but his observation assured me that Eddie was sharper than he looked. His plaid shirt and jeans gave the impression that he was an ordinary guy, but his sharp eyes and the way he handled the gun told me he was competent. Customs hadn't given me much of a problem since I filled out the relevant paperwork to declare the Walther Q5 Match in my luggage. Now, Bessie, as I dubbed the Walther, was strapped to my ankle.

Eddie's phone beeped and he looked at the display. "Bhavin is almost back at the café. Let's go."

I got to my feet, adrenaline pumping through my veins at the potential action to come. "Let's hope he's on the up and up and isn't messing us around."

Our walk back to the café was accomplished in half the time. Bhavin came from the opposite direction as we approached the door. We waited on the sidewalk. The evening peak-hour traffic moved like molasses. Impatient motorists blasted their horns at other drivers as soon as the stoplight changed.

The uncertain smile pasted on Bhavin's face and the guile in his eyes raised my antenna. His feet shuffled on the concrete as Eddie told him we were ready for him to lead us to Myers.

Bhavin folded his arms and puffed up his chest. "I need you to pay me more to tell you where deh have him."

Eddie glowered at him. "We agreed on a price and that's what I'm paying. Not a dollar more."

They haggled for a bit while I grew more annoyed with each second that passed. The heat and humidity didn't help. This unreliable snitch was taking up valuable time. In another hour or so, night would be on us. I wanted to complete this assignment and get back to the woman who now seemed to have me body and soul even when she was nowhere in proximity.

I stepped between both men. “Here’s what we’re gonna do. Bhavin, you can go. Eddie and I will find Myers on our own.”

Bhavin’s eyes went wide and he squawked. “Yuh have to pay me because I already proved dat I saw di American man. I can help yuh find him, too.”

“Listen.” I moved closer and stared down at him. “We don’t have to do squat. You haven’t given us anything worth paying you a dime. Make up your mind. Either you know where Myers is or you don’t.”

“I...I—”

“You know what I think?” I exchanged a glance with Eddie. “Bhavin here is just playing with us. I say we turn him upside down and shake the truth out of him.”

Bhavin eyes bulged, and before Eddie or I could do anything, he took off running down the street.

six

THAT SNITCH RUNNING AWAY ANNOYED me more than anything else. More time wasted while we chased his scuzzy behind for no good reason. I broke the corner and cut my speed.

Bhavin was sprawled on the sidewalk along with the old woman he'd knocked to the ground. Several women threatened Bhavin with raised voices and hot glares.

I hauled him to his feet, while Eddie assisted the old lady with gathering her handbag and umbrella.

Bhavin twisted to get out of my grip as we walked past other curious passers-by.

As soon as Eddie caught up with us, we walked Bhavin to the silver Nissan Note parked close to the café. By now, night was falling. Eddie took the wheel and I sat in the back with Bhavin, who whined about getting his money.

"You have to give me something before you get something," Eddie snarled from the driver's seat.

"You hear that?" I looked sideways at him. "You better start talking before I get really annoyed with you. My time is important and you've already wasted enough of it."

"Turn right at the corner," he said, with resentment dripping from his voice.

Within five minutes, we were at the foot of the entrance of the Laventille. The small, colorful houses perched on a hillside as if a giant's hand had dropped them in a hodgepodge formation. In the densely populated area, the houses were arranged in tiers until they seemed to touch the clouds above us. The narrow streets would be a problem if we had to run for our lives. In many low-income communities, I noticed that people the world over tended to gather outside their houses, passing the time. This place was different. In fact, the silence was deafening, the atmosphere so tense, I hesitated to speak but had to ask, "Where is everybody?"

"In their houses." Eddie's tone was grim. "The murder rate around here is high, so..."

He didn't have to say more. I understood. We got out of the car and continued on foot. Eddie kept a firm grip on Bhavin, who became even less cooperative than before.

"What about di money?" he asked, while Eddie hustled up a steep, winding lane packed with houses.

"You know how to reach me," Eddie said. "Plus, you know you won't get a dollar unless your info is good."

"But, boss, you know I never let you down."

"Right."

They walked ahead of me and couldn't hear my soft chuckle. Earlier, I asked Eddie why he used Bhavin if he was so unreliable. His answer was that Bhavin knew everybody, had a nose for people's business, and was accurate eighty-five percent of the time. I hoped we wouldn't be in the other fifteen percent in this life-and-death situation.

Eddie's raised hand stopped me after his hushed conversation with Bhavin. "Remember you nah get no pay if yuh information wrong."

Bhavin's furious whisper carried to me. "Dis is where dey have him up to last night."

"Just remember what I said."

The moment Eddie released Bhavin, he took off like a monkey with its tail on fire. In seconds, he disappeared under the sparse street lights.

Eddie pointed to a house two doors up from where we stood. The building was dark and still, with paint flaking from the walls. If Myers and his captors were inside, why did the house seem uninhabited?

We put on the gloves Eddie supplied, then he slipped the Ruger out of his waist. He beckoned me forward as he approached the front of the house and told me his plan.

The Walther in my hand gave me a sense of security although something told me this evening wouldn't work out to be a win. Bhavin's reaction also didn't bode well for a good outcome. I stood back and Eddie moved toward the front door, which didn't look as if it needed more than a puff of wind to blow it down. One side kick from him left the door flat on the ground.

I covered him, aided by a tiny flashlight with a powerful beam. We cleared all the corners of the small room, avoiding the scene in the center. Between us, we checked the two bedrooms and a tiny kitchen before we came back to the living room. The space was bare, with the exception of a rickety chair, a broken-down sofa, and piles of trash. A man was slumped in a ladder-back chair in the middle of the room, his hands and ankles bound and his shirt half open.

With the beam of the flashlight guiding me, I walked around him, careful not to disturb the bits of rubble around our feet. From the electrical cable on the wooden floor and the metal prod attached, I could make an accurate guess as to what happened. He'd been electrocuted to death by someone who didn't know what the hell they were doing. The man's facial features confirmed he was Duran Myers.

"The next time I see that little fart, I'm going to beat the shit out of him." With that comment, Eddie grunted and spun out of the room.

When I caught up with him, he gestured toward the house. "I hate seeing a life wasted like that. It's like they couldn't wait to get that ransom or access to the pharmaceuticals Moray thinks they wanted. They just dumped him and probably moved on to some other unfortunate soul already."

"Yes. For some, life is just a game where everything comes down to the survival of the fittest."

We didn't waste any time leaving the crime scene. As we walked with brisk steps, we pulled off the gloves and stuffed them into our pockets and thankfully didn't encounter anything other than stray dogs on our way out of the community.

While we sat in the car, Eddie placed a call to the police station and reported what we found. Although I never stuck around when the person I went in to extract was dead, I questioned him about the implications of us leaving a crime scene, then making a report. He explained that he worked closely with the police, so it wouldn't be a major challenge.

"Better to get out of Laventille than to stay and possibly be attacked by the residents for something we haven't done." He slid a glance sideways. "Around here, things turn volatile in the blink of an eye."

Before he switched on the car engine, Eddie let out a deep breath. "I have a son his age. It just kills me when people commit senseless acts like we just saw. It's a pointless waste of that man's life. Why run the risk of killing him when they already waited a week?"

"Sometimes, I think access to technology and our insatiable lust for money has done us more harm than good." I shrugged. "My guess is that they got tired of waiting, plus a bit too enthusiastic with punishing him."

"You're probably right." Eddie moved his head from side to side. "Kidnapping people for money has turned this island upside down. Crime is out of control and the police don't have enough manpower to maintain law and order."

We didn't speak on the ten-minute ride back to my hotel. When

Eddie stopped the Nissan, he shook my hand. "I wish we'd met under better circumstances, but we can't change how this unfolded."

"Yes. I wish I had better news for Ralph, too."

I got out, thankful to return from Laventille with no injuries. In this line of work, you never knew.

The moment I got to my room, I rang Ralph to update him on the situation. He thanked me and after fifteen minutes we were finished.

My next step was to book a flight back home.

After that, I rehashed the day, thinking about where I could have improved on any aspect of the job. Most of the time, I ended up bringing home the people I was hired to find. Today was a reminder that the job didn't always come to a satisfactory conclusion. Sometimes, the things I saw made me sick to my stomach and I had to channel my mind along more pleasant avenues. This was one such time.

After a long, hot shower I propped myself against the headboard, watching the international news. By then, enough time had passed for me to shut out the pictures of that miserable little house in Laventille and Myers's lifeless body.

At times, when it was impossible to get the day's events out of my head, I studied financial reports, researched business trends, or meditated until I was back to being myself. Each time I did an extraction, I talked to Corinne only after decompressing and compartmentalizing my thoughts. As best I could, I kept what I did on these assignments separate from her.

Corinne was like a refreshing sea breeze brushing my skin after I came away disgusted from the situations I encountered in the field. Her insistence on knowing how I was doing mentally and physically, whenever we were apart, plus her lively conversation sprinkled with soft laughter, reminded me of all that was good about having a special woman in my life.

I called twice before she answered. "You've surfaced, huh?"

"Hey, sweets, how are you?" I lowered the sound on the television and dropped the remote on the bed.

"You sure you're talking to the right woman? There's nothing sweet about me."

"Let me be the judge of that." I thought about what I wanted to say next and before I convinced myself not to say the words, I blurted, "I've missed you like crazy, Corinne."

"Really?" The throaty chuckle that hit my ear made me smile, until she said, "If you missed me, you'd be here with me getting some of this mmm-mmm goodness."

"You're wrong for teasing me like that." Frowning, I asked, "Speaking of which, where are you now?"

She chuckled again, but I wasn't sure she was actually amused. "Where did you promise to meet me?"

"Woman, stop being difficult and tell me if you're still where I think you are. I can call my mother or my brother and find out if you're where I left you, so I don't know why we're having this conversation."

"I don't know either." A pause dropped between us before she continued. "To tell the truth, I also don't know why I'm still in Antigua waiting for you like some groupie."

She didn't mean that as a compliment, but I laughed. "I think I should be offended, but I also believe you've just paid me a back-handed compliment."

"Take it whatever way you like."

"Despite your sauciness, I still look forward to seeing you tomorrow."

Her response was quick and carried a slight sting. "I'll look for you with one eye."

"You better be at that airport waiting for me tomorrow night." I heaved a dramatic sigh for effect. "D'you know how many flights I've had to scroll through to make it from here to there in one day?"

Corinne went silent, and when I wondered if the call had dropped, she asked, "Mind telling me where *here* is? You didn't tell me where you were going when you left."

"Trinidad and Tobago."

"Hmmm."

"What does that mean? I don't think you understand how much I want to be with you."

"No, love, but you can tell me if you happen to turn up."

She'd stuck me with another barb, but I didn't remark on it. Since we started seeing each other more regularly in the last year, I had instances where I surfaced a day later than we were supposed to meet. Rarely, it happened that I had back-to-back jobs and was forced to disappoint her. This time, no matter what happened, I'd return to Antigua like I promised.

If Corinne allowed us to move in the direction I wanted, it wouldn't be difficult to turn my back on this part of my life. What I did from this point depended on her. I hoped she'd be willing to meet me halfway, even with my shortcomings.

seven

A DAY after I arrived in Antigua, Doug and Khalila left for their home in Miami. Corinne and I had Mama's two-bedroom beach cottage to ourselves. We used the time to relax, talking for hours on end, playing board games, and roaming the beach. I wouldn't have missed that interlude with her for anything.

Marcus Larmond's phone call ended an interlude that was the most memorable I'd had with any woman in many years. Corinne and I flew into Miami yesterday afternoon and had dinner with Doug and Khalila. For at least another week or two, Corinne would be with them.

After Larmond's call, I gave her the impression I was travelling out of state and would be back in a day or so. Better to have that buffer just in case the job took longer than I anticipated.

When I told Corinne I was leaving, she said, "This time with you was too good to be true. You better thank your lucky stars Khalila and I have a spa day planned for tomorrow." After studying me for a full minute, she shook her head and abandoned her space next to me in the hanging loveseat on the back patio. At the doorway, she put up two fingers, less than a half inch apart. "I'm this close to giving up on you and your bullshit."

I stared at the paving stones, telling myself I was a fool for not taking my brother's advice to simply tell Corinne what I did when I wasn't with her.

My regret followed me to my present location, and a sniffle brought me back to where I sat.

The dark, burly man looking at me across the coffee table wasn't overly worried. But the light-skinned woman next to him carried enough anxiety for both of them. She had a strong connection to the boy they asked me to find. Him, not so much.

She dabbed her eyes with the crumpled tissue she blew her nose with a moment ago. I understood and excused her. Angella had fallen apart twice in the ten minutes we'd been talking. My gaze went to the elegant furnishings in their apartment while I gave her time to compose herself.

She sounded stuffy when she was able to speak. "Please find him, Mr. Blythe."

I'll do my best." I picked up the photo of the sixteen-year-old boy who resembled Angella. "You'll get an update as soon as I have anything to report."

With the information they gave me, it wouldn't be difficult to find the teenager.

"We transferred the funds to your account earlier today." Marcus Larmond sounded as if the thought pained him.

It wasn't necessary to say I wouldn't have been meeting with them otherwise. Time and wisdom taught me to collect my fees before I started any job. I'd been burned once or twice in the past. Today, my reputation spoke for me. I didn't negotiate fees. Whatever I quoted was what I expected to be paid.

Looking into Larmond's eyes confirmed that he was detached from this process. I wondered why.

"Is Jace your biological son?"

He shook his head. "Doesn't matter though," he said, putting an arm around Angella. "We just want him back."

My half-smile was as fake as his words, but I didn't have to like him to complete the task they gave me. I picked up my phone off the coffee table and met his eyes. "You sound Jamaican. That's where you're from?"

He nodded and forced a smile as if small talk was beyond him. "I hear the Caribbean in you, too."

"Antigua," I said, by way of an explanation.

"I contacted you through an associate who told me you're good at what you do. He's originally from Antigua."

I acknowledged his comment by dipping my head. "I try to satisfy my clients."

Larmond walked me to the door, and when I stood on the other side of the threshold, I turned away, then spun back as if I'd forgotten something. "D'you have any children?"

Eyes narrowed, he asked, "Why d'you want to know?"

I shrugged, as if his answer didn't matter. "You don't sound very invested in this process."

After he threw a glance over his shoulder, he stepped into the corridor and lowered his voice. "The boy is spoiled rotten. And to be truthful, I'm not good with kids."

"So that's a yes on not having children?"

"I came close but..."

Marcus seemed to be stuck, so I prompted him because I wanted to know more. "What happened?"

"I...we lost a child and I didn't know how to handle it, so I walked away. That was many years ago when I was back home."

His shook his head as if coming out of a fog. "My apologies. I don't even know why I brought that up."

I kept the distaste off my face because it wasn't my place to judge. Still, I couldn't help wondering what kind of man walked away from a woman who needed him when she'd lost part of herself. A pang of regret filled my throat. Conversations like these always resurrected unpleasant memories.

"Don't worry about it." I held out my hand to him.

Marcus shook it and gave me a genuine smile. “See what you can do about Jace. I don’t think Angella could bear losing him.”

“I’ll do my best.”

My past—my own memories of losing a child—threatened to knock at the door of my consciousness, but I suppressed those thoughts and focused my energy on how I was going to retrieve their son, who had gotten involved with a group of small-time criminals.

On my way out of their apartment building, I got hold of my partner, Neil McLeish. We’d been part of the The Royal Antigua and Barbuda Defence Force, one of the smallest military outfits in the world. Among my specialties had been the prevention of drug smuggling and search and rescue missions. My natural affinity for the latter wasn’t my first choice as a career path after I left the army. I wanted to see more of the world and started by island hopping in the Caribbean. My visits to Grenada, the spice island, and Jamaica, producer of world-renowned Blue Mountain coffee, started a love affair that eventually became a business. The market in Europe for Caribbean spices and coffee ensured that I stayed busy.

I stumbled into extracting people when I met Neil while on vacation and visiting relatives in Florida. He asked me to help with rescuing a child from her father, who was in a custody battle with her mother. From there, Neil and I partnered up months later for another job, and I continued going to diverse places to move people to safety under various conditions.

We didn’t have an official base, but kept a server where everything was digitized and which we both accessed, as needed. Our directors’ meetings happened wherever we operated together on an assignment. We also kept an apartment in Miami, which we used to house our clients whenever necessary. When it wasn’t in use and I was in town, I stayed there. That’s where I went after leaving Corinne at Doug’s home. I shut off my thoughts and speed dialed Neil’s number.

“What d’you need?” His voice sounded crisp and clear despite it being almost dusk.

"Are you free for a meeting at Liberty City in an hour?"

"Sounds doable. What's the situation?"

I filled in the details in a half-dozen sentences. "Before that, I need to make a stop at the apartment. I'll meet you at the location his mother thinks he's hanging around."

"Sounds like a plan. See you then."

The good thing about working alongside someone with Neil's skill set was that I didn't need to tell him to come prepared. We'd done this often enough that he knew what was required.

* * *

Neil's booted foot hit the rickety door with a force that smashed the wood against the wall inside the back door. We rushed through the kitchen, our combat boots thundering on the wooden floorboards.

Our voices competed with the gunshots and shouts coming from the television in one corner. "Don't Move! Get your hands up! Now!"

Two of the men in the untidy living room sprang to attention, but their eyes were glazed, as if our commands confused them. The other two abandoned their seats and sprinted toward the front door. Only one stayed where he lay on the sofa.

"Stop, or I will shoot." Neil's words were terse and commanding.

The men rushed the door and scrabbled to get it open. Their clumsy efforts amused me and I exchanged a glance with Neil, who shook his head. I was certain the mask he wore hid a grin.

The two jokers trying to avoid us were stoned out of their minds and couldn't have found water in a well. Dressed as we were, they probably thought we had materialized from the manufactured garbage they'd been watching on the television.

The pungent haze in the air confirmed the boys had been smoking weed. When they stopped wrestling with the lock that wouldn't cooperate with their clumsy efforts to escape, they faced us with their hands up and their eyes pulled wide.

"Step away from the door." I motioned with the gun for them to cooperate.

They did as instructed, then the one with nut-brown skin asked. "What d'you want?"

I scanned the room, noting the pizza boxes piled on one table and the lines of white powder on top of a glass coffee table covered with dust. With my phone, I snapped several pictures of the table and the teenagers across the room.

"Which one of you is Carey?"

"He ain't here," the second guy with his hands in the air said. "Who are you?"

"Don't worry about who we are." After glancing at the table, my attention returned to him. "Worry about the problems you'll have with the police when we turn you over to them."

"Don't pay any attention to them. They ain't law enforcement." This from the direction of the largest sofa, where a young man sprawled on the cushion. A good look at him confirmed he was Jace. The curly hair and low fade matched the picture his mother showed me.

I didn't want him alerted to our end game, so I said, "You certainly know a lot for someone who's high as a kite."

He sprang to his feet. "For your information—"

I pointed my Walther Q5 Match at Jace. "Sit and shut up."

He complied but threw a resentful glare my way.

"Put your hands down." The teens complied while I asked, "When d'you expect Carey back?"

Jace's gaze was shifty when he answered. "I don't know. He didn't—"

"Don't say another word." Neil waved the Glock 24 to indicate he meant business.

We exchanged a look amd then our attention went to the front door, which opened from the outside. A bearded man dressed in a T-shirt, jacket, and jeans stepped across the threshold. He threw a cautious glance over his shoulder before shutting the door behind him. When he realized we were holding his friends at gunpoint, he shuffled backward and reached for his waist.

"Don't do it." Neil trained his weapon on the guy, who immediately raised both hands above his head.

I crossed the linoleum floor, walked around him, and removed the gun from the back of his waist. The serial number had been filed off the Sig Sauer P938, which I slipped into my waistband for safekeeping.

His fierce growl would have made me more cautious of him if the fear in his eyes wasn't obvious.

"Carey?"

"Who wants to know?" he asked, his stance combative.

I pointed to the kitchen with the Walther. "I need to have a word with you in there."

His gaze went to the weapon, then shot back to meet mine.

"Don't worry." My voice was cold when I added, "I don't plan to harm you...this time."

He shrank back, then recovered his bravado and scowled.

His initial reaction satisfied me. Neil and I made an intimidating sight dressed in black from head to feet, including the ski masks that hid our faces.

"Follow me."

I didn't wait to see whether he obeyed or not. Neil's hulking presence and ominous silence said more than any words I could have uttered. Inside the kitchen, I faced Carey. His dark-brown eyes flickered with uncertainty, and I did nothing to make him think I wouldn't turn on him at any minute.

The racket from the television intruded as I walked a slow circle around him. When I stopped, my gaze wandered around the space as if I was alone. The kitchen was in no better condition than the living room, with dishes piled high in the sink and the floor sticky under my feet.

I felt him watching me and when he moved from one foot to another, I stared him in the eyes. He was in his mid-twenties and the oldest of the lot. Carey's shifting expressions told me he'd been in this position a time or two. No doubt with the police and perhaps rival gangs. At his age, and with his experience, he could prey on the youngsters under his influence. Neil had looked him up before we descended on the house. Carey was small time, looking to go big on the backs of the vulnerable.

Lifting my chin toward the living room, I said, "See that boy in there? I mean Jace."

He nodded, but a spark of defiance lit his eyes.

"As of now, you're going to pretend you don't know him." I let that sink in. "I hear you've been trying to recruit him for your business."

Neil's intel revealed that Carey was into selling weed and had linked up with Jamaicans thought to be involved in lottery scamming, which was big business in the underworld.

"What if I am? And what if I told you he came to me?" Carey jammed one thumb to his chest.

I stepped in close and lowered my voice. "Like I said, forget you ever knew him. Even if he speaks to you after today, you're going to act as if you've never laid eyes on him in your life. You understand?"

He held my gaze but refused to answer. Then his eyes gleamed. "Who is he to you, anyway?"

"That's not your business."

"Oh, so it's okay for a stranger to come into my space and demand that I hand over someone I've invested in and just let him walk away?" As he spoke, Carey regained confidence. He shook his head. "Nah, man. That's not right."

"Understand this. I'm not here to negotiate."

"What do I get out of this?"

My answer was swift. "Nothing."

Carey pulled his head back. "Are you for real, man?"

I lifted my hand to bring the gun into view. "As real as the pain this Walther brings when it's discharged in your flesh."

The threat brought back the reality of his situation and he folded his arms. “I don’t scare easy.”

“That’s not what I’m trying to do. I’m giving you facts. If you don’t back off, expect another visit from us. And, if we have to come back, you won’t get off this easy.”

Carey’s face twisted but he didn’t open his mouth.

The pores in his face were visible when I stood in his space. “Did. You. Hear. Me?”

After a battle of wills that had Carey lowering his gaze, he huffed and stepped back. “I hear you. I don’t need no trouble.”

“No, you don’t.”

“I’m going to need my gun back.”

“Do I look stupid to you?”

I stepped aside and let him return to the room where the boys sat on the sofa watching Neil. With one finger, I beckoned to Jace. “You’re coming with me.”

“I don’t know you, man. I’m not going nowhere with you.”

He hissed and mumbled until my glare silenced him. “I’m not going to tell you twice.”

Jace looked at Carey as if he wanted him to intervene but Carey fixed his attention on the table in the center of the room. The muscles in his jaw worked, and I imagined how powerless he felt letting his recruit walk out the door, but we had the advantage.

I gripped Jace by the arm and led him out the way we came in. When he realized we were leaving, he resisted me. “What’s wrong with you? I ain’t done nothin’. This is abuse. Where you taking me?”

He continued spouting questions that I had no intention of answering until we had some privacy.

After leaving the group inside with a warning, Neil came down the steps behind me and slid into the driver’s side of the Honda Civic, then pulled away from the sidewalk.

In the back seat, I explained to Jace what he would and wouldn’t be doing in the coming weeks, along with the consequences he’d face if he stepped out of line. I didn’t take pleasure in scaring him, but it was my experience that some kids took a lot more convincing than others to stay on the right path. His resentful silence didn't matter. His safety and wellbeing did.

That brought me satisfaction. His mother would be happy to have her son back and hopefully, she'd get him the help he needed. If Jace wanted a future, he'd take heed and act right.

Neil gave me a half-smile in the rearview mirror and I winked at him. If only half the jobs we did were this easy. Now, I was free to get back to Doug's place to finish my business with Corinne. For half a second, my stomach dropped at the thought that I wouldn't ever be able to convince Corinne to be mine exclusively.

I didn't think she was seeing anyone else, but I'd make it my business to ensure she was my woman only. Twenty-four hours apart and Corinne danced all over my mind nonstop. We had a dinner date for Saturday evening and I'd make sure that date was special.

Meantime, I planned to catch up on everything I'd been neglecting because of my travels. My executive assistant, based in London, was efficient and stayed on top of the distribution end of the business for Blythe Distributors. Douglas was my partner in the company and liaised with our accountant each week to keep our finances in order.

My musing stopped when Jace shifted and glared at me. As soon as we returned him to his mother, I'd go over the sales and distribution reports that waited for my attention. I wanted my plate clear of all business matters by noon tomorrow. If anything else came up, Neil would have to handle it on his own.

eight

I FELT like the luckiest man alive sitting across from Corinne. Saturday morning came and went with me analyzing the reports my assistant, Beth, submitted electronically. I was rested and in a great mood. Tonight, I planned to make love to Corinne until she begged me to stop.

My hand was wrapped around my wine glass when Marcus Larmond's face came into view over Corinne's shoulder. He'd come from the back of the room, most likely the washroom, and sat several tables away. Only God knew how I missed him until now.

His eyes met mine, then his gaze drifted to the back of Corinne's head. He stiffened and I knew the moment the thought of coming to our table formed in his mind. Business was about to intrude on my personal time if I didn't head Larmond off his current track. A killing stare did not keep him in his seat. He excused himself from his live-in-lover, Angella, and sauntered toward us.

The cool jazz I'd been enjoying a minute ago turned into white noise as he came closer. If luck was on my side, he wouldn't say anything to send Corinne's curiosity into overdrive. I wanted nothing more than to sweep Corinne out of the Mediterranean restaurant she'd insisted she wanted to try, but we were in the middle of our meal.

Corinne picked up her wine glass and tipped one eyebrow. "You okay, Roger?"

I stabbed a shrimp and forked it into my mouth, wanting to impale Marcus, who arrived at our table at that moment. Ignoring him obviously wouldn't make him disappear, so I laid down the fork and prepared to stand.

Corinne took one look at Larmond, placed her glass on the table, and wiped her lips with a napkin. Her actions were sluggish yet deliberate. I wasn't sure what was happening, but the sick sensation in my stomach told me nothing good would come from the interaction between Corinne and Larmond.

"What a surprise," Larmond said, feigning shock, as if I hadn't just watched him raking Corinne with his gaze like she was a delicacy he couldn't wait to sample. "Corinne?"

She stared him up and down. "You," she said in a quiet, frosty voice. Then, cool as you please, Corinne stood and flung the contents of her water glass in his face.

When the ice and water hit him, Larmond gasped and backed up a few inches. He spluttered, while Corinne turned her gaze on me as if daring me to ask any questions.

"Corinne!" Larmond stood with his mouth open in disbelief.

The people at the tables around us stared openly, but they were the least of my concern. My attention came back to Corinne when she said, "Don't you dare speak to me." She shot Larmond a glare, then turned fiery eyes on me. "If this man doesn't get the hell away from us, I'm leaving."

I didn't have confirmation, but suspected what was unfolding before my eyes. Corinne was the woman from Larmond's past. With fury simmering in my gut, I snapped, "You heard the lady."

A waiter rushed over and hovered next to Larmond as if unsure what to do next.

"But—" Larmond wiped his face and continued talking to Corinne.

"Roger." Corinne's voice shook as she pulled in a breath, then collapsed in her seat. Her skin was ashen and she sounded strained when she looked up at Larmond. "Please make him go away."

I stood and gestured toward the entrance. "Larmond, you heard what she said."

Instead of leaving, he raised both hands. "All I—"

"I don't want to hear it." I gripped his upper arm and moved him away from the table. He was testing my patience. Between Corinne's reaction to him and his explanation when I met with him and Angella, I was floored. Corinne was the woman he'd left when she lost their child.

The diners around us abandoned their food to watch our drama. The floor manager appeared at my elbow at the same time the waiter returned with a mop.

I couldn't keep the scorn out of my voice when I addressed Larmond in the foyer. "Obviously, you don't understand the woman you were with."

His lips pulled away from his teeth in a snarl. "And you think you know her better than I do?" He raised both brows and threw a glance over his shoulder. "We were together for five years. How long have *you* known her?"

"That's none of your blasted business. What is this? A competition? You should be ashamed of your damn self."

After shoving him through the doorway, I stood next to him on the sidewalk. My voice rose to compete with the traffic. "Does it matter how long I've known Corinne? What matters is that I now have the woman you threw away, and if I have anything to do with it, Corinne and I will be together in the foreseeable future."

He winced, as if I hit him. "I'm sure if I got a chance to explain—"

I stepped aside to allow a couple to enter the restaurant and once more pitched my voice above the traffic going in both directions. "You have a nerve, you know that? You saw her reaction to you.

Corinne was well rid of you. If you don't want me knocking down your door, you'd better not contact her."

"What can you do about it?" he asked, pulling the wet shirt away from his chest. Larmond opened his mouth, then shut it when Angella burst through the door and gripped his arm. "Marcus, I had to pay the bill since you left without me. Why did that woman throw water at you?"

He eased the shirt off his chest again. "It's a long story that I prefer not to talk about right now."

She frowned, pushing the hair away from her face. "But—"

"I said I don't want to talk about it." He took her arm and walked her down the street as if I didn't exist. A moment later, Angella tugged her hand out of his and marched away.

I stared after them, rubbing the back of my neck while trying to make sense of the last fifteen minutes.

Corinne was tough, or so she told herself, but that man had done some serious damage, and I expected to take a pummeling from her after the cruel hand fate had just dealt her. She lashed out when she was hurt and I'd gotten used to her coping mechanism because I had let her down too many times with my absences.

What was the likelihood that the woman I wanted had history with a client of mine? Very likely, it seemed.

I walked back inside to find her picking up her purse, as if she intended to leave without me. Staring through me, she said, "I'd like to go home."

Platitudes wouldn't help this situation, so I simply nodded and took her hand in mine. Her skin was cold, as if the season was winter rather than springtime. I tried to gauge her mood, but it was hard to tell with Corinne. This incident was way outside any other shared experience we'd had so far.

She kept her head high and eyes focused in front of her.

I waited until we drove off in the Chrysler I kept in Miami before I spoke. "Are you going to tell me what that was all about?"

"No."

We stopped at a light and I glanced across at her. "No?"

"You heard me the first time." She looked at me as if she hated me, but I also realized her eyes were glossy. I'd never seen her tear up before. A weight dropped on my shoulders and descended to my chest. Then it sat in my belly. I wasn't the smartest man in the world, but it didn't take much to figure out that I wouldn't be getting any information out of her tonight.

The traffic was light, so we arrived back at Doug's house in ten minutes. I switched off the engine and prepared to get out of the car.

Corinne's icy voice stopped me. "Roger, I'd prefer if you didn't stay the night."

Her words had the effect of a brick hitting me in the stomach. I figured if she didn't want to talk or make love with me, at least I could wrap my arms around her and offer my support. We had an unspoken agreement that I'd spend tonight with her.

"Corinne—"

"I won't argue about it. Please, just do what I ask."

I pulled in a deep breath. "What you're saying is, you refuse to talk about what has you in this state. That I'm to ignore what you did at the restaurant and act as if nothing happened."

"Exactly."

"That's just—"

"What I want. And I'd be grateful if you'd respect my wishes." She shoved the door of the Chrysler open.

I was on my feet in a flash and met her on the sidewalk. Gently, I gripped her arms to get her to connect with me. "Corinne—"

She pulled her shoulders back and looked somewhere over my shoulder. Under the streetlight, her face was blank. Her attitude was matter-of-fact. Wearing a slight smile, she said, "Right now, I have nothing to say, nothing to give. Nothing you do will convince me to share anything. Just give me some space. When I'm ready to talk to you, I'll call."

I searched her eyes. They were as cold as her voice. Her expression hardened under my gaze. Corinne meant every word she said.

Despite knowing she was in pain, I let her go. There was no way I could tell her I knew what happened between her and Larmond.

So many of her quirks now made sense—her reluctance to have deep conversations, her flippancy when I needed her to be serious, and her attitude toward relationships. I was well aware Corinne was no angel. We were honest with each other about the way we lived our lives. Now, we were settling into a groove I was comfortable with and couldn't have anticipated this setback.

As she walked toward the front door, I leaned against the car and racked my brain for a way to show her I cared, and that I'd be there for her no matter what that asshole had done to her.

nine

KHALILA WAS RIGHT. You never quite get over the hurt of being betrayed. The forgiveness part was what I still hadn't mastered. That's what drove me to take my hurt out on Roger, who I was sure intuitively understood what had happened between Marcus and me. I had loved that man with everything in me, and he disappointed me.

Big time.

Seeing him had been like having my body cut open without anesthetic. After the initial shock, I wanted to leap on him and tear him to shreds. Only the decorum I learned over the years stopped me from creating a bigger scene inside that upscale restaurant.

To his credit, Roger had left me alone when I turned unpleasant and uncommunicative. I had a host of questions for him, like how he knew Marcus. He'd addressed him by name, and I was also curious to know what they'd been talking about after they left the restaurant. The two of them were out there too long to be having anything but a discussion that concerned me.

Roger had been reluctant to leave, but my cruel words finally got through to him. I didn't want to be mean, but if I didn't make him leave, I'd break down, and I didn't need to share the humiliating part of my life with him. I'd been through the hurt and upheaval a thousand times, examining why I wasn't woman enough for Marcus to stick around. Why after planning to build a future together, I was no longer good enough for him because I couldn't have children.

When the hemorrhaging wouldn't stop after Nadia was born, the doctor gave my mother and Marcus two options. Remove my uterus or take the chance that I might stop bleeding before I was too weak to survive. Marcus had been a mess and incapable of giving any input. My mother made the decision to save my life.

At the time we weren't married, which was just as well. Surviving a divorce, as well as dealing with his abandonment, would have destroyed me.

I was grateful to be alive, but after Marcus left there were days when I considered why I should even bother to go on. But I'd never been someone to wallow in self-pity, so I had borne the loss of Nadia alone, except for Khalila and my mother who were there every step of the way.

While I knew Roger was only trying to comfort me, I didn't want to share something that I'd buried so deep it would be excruciating to dig it up. Sleep had been elusive and last night I lay in bed looking all over the room, rehashing my time with Marcus. Then I thought about the way I'd lived over the last ten years before my thoughts turned to Roger.

Seeing Marcus reminded me of all the reasons I never immersed myself totally in any man's life. Roger had breached the wall I'd erected around my emotions and my heart and I didn't like it one bit, even though it was obvious that I mattered to him. If I didn't, he wouldn't make the effort to stay in touch when he was away and he certainly wouldn't be insisting that we spend more time together.

When my thoughts wouldn't stop delaying sleep, I grabbed my phone and scrolled through hundreds of baby pictures until my eyelids were too heavy to stay open.

Khalila and I had made plans to go shopping today, but I couldn't make myself get out of bed. After another twenty minutes, I showered and sat before the mirror. I loosed my hair and recaptured it at the back of my neck. Then I changed my mind again and let it hang loose. Maybe my tired eyes wouldn't be so obvious. After making the bed, I sat on the edge of it, staring around the room. Khalila had done a fabulous job of decorating their home. This bedroom had a cream-and-brown theme going on, which included the bed, drapery, carpet, and love seat.

I went to the window and stood there, thinking that even the garden was well-tended. Thanks to Doug. Both of them cooperated to make their marriage, home, and family life work. Even to the point of doing the necessities to ensure his daughters and Khalila found some mutual ground, despite a rocky start to their relationship and grievances on both sides.

It would be wonderful having that kind of synergy with someone, but I hadn't been able to bring myself to dream of what life would look like with Roger at my side. I was a coward, but with good cause. My negative thoughts demanded that I lay back down.

A tap sounded at the door and when I answered, Khalila pushed it open. "Are you okay?"

Avoiding her gaze, I asked, "Why would you think I'm not all right?"

She walked in with Zane propped on her hip. "Because you're an early riser, and I haven't heard a peep out of you this morning."

"It's only half past eight."

"That's my point." She perched on the bed and sat Zane beside her. He crawled toward me, making his usual gurgling sounds. I sat up and scooped him into my lap. Over his head, I met Khalila's eyes. "I saw Marcus last night."

I counted to seven in my head before Khalila opened her mouth. "Did you say Marcus?"

"Are you getting deaf in your old age?"

She frowned while studying me as if I was about to die. "Uh, no, but ... where? How?"

I gave her the run down, then added, "He had the nerve to act as if I'd ever want to see him in this life again."

Letting out an audible breath, she said, "Maybe he thought you'd forgiven him after all this time."

"I'd be more likely to forgive someone of murdering my mother than excuse him for what he did."

Zane looked up at me with one fist crammed into his mouth, and I loosened my hold on him.

After a long sigh, Khalila cleared her throat. "I'm not going to give you my usual spiel about what unforgiveness does to the body. All I'm going to say is that you've done a fine job of living without him all these years. You have something great with Roger, don't allow Marcus to derail all that."

"Who says I'm gonna let that happen?"

With both eyebrows elevated, Khalila asked, "Do I need to remind you that I know the havoc you're capable of wreaking when you try?"

"Really? That's all you have?"

Khalila pulled back, frowning. "All I have? Have you forgotten how you called Jeff's wife and told her that he was having an affair?"

While stroking Zane's soft hair, I said, "Jeff should have told me he was married before he got into my bed."

"Agreed, but—"

"But nothing, Khalila. When I found out, he refused to leave me alone. I had no choice after he kept badgering me."

Her nostrils flared and she shook her head but Khalila's expression softened when she looked at Zane. A gleam came to her eyes and she chuckled. "There was no excuse for putting Miguel's things next to his car—in the middle of the street—and soaking them with water..."

"He was cheating."

Khalila gave me an incredulous look. "How does that excuse qualify? You wouldn't even admit you were having a relationship with him. It's no wonder he felt he could do his own thing."

“I may flit around, but I have standards. In all this time, I didn’t step out on any of them. Miguel should have known better.”

“The man needed something deeper and you refused to do more than go out with him and have sex. I hate to tell you, but even men need commitment at some point in their lives.”

“That’s perfectly all right.” I rested my chin on Zane’s head and wriggled it around. “Miguel wasn’t the one. He knew it and I knew it. We were just passing time with each other.”

Khalila raised both hands. “I give you that, but I hope you hang in there with Roger. Marcus is so far in your past, he shouldn’t matter. You know how I feel about not letting go of all the hurt. It poisons the soul.”

I brushed aside her comments because I didn’t want to deal with that issue. After pressing a kiss to Zane’s head, I lifted him so he stood on my thighs. “D’you remember the talk we had about the stuff on my bucket list that hasn’t happened yet?”

Khalila’s tone was cautious when she answered. “Uh-huh.”

“Well, I think it’s time for me to take some action.”

Zane clapped his hands once as if he agreed with me.

Amusement lit Khalila’s eyes. “Don’t tell me you’re aiming to swim across the Black River with those crocodiles in it.”

“I don’t have a death wish.” I chided her with my gaze. “If I recall correctly, I said rafting on the Rio Grande.”

“I’m sure you said something about swimming someplace,” Khalila grumbled.

“Just not in the Black River. Now if I got a chance to shove Marcus overboard while on safari there…”

Khalila laughed. “You’re going to burn in hell for thinking that.”

“And you’ll be right beside me for giggling about taking a man’s life.”

“Seriously though,” Khalila said, tipping her head sideways. “What are you planning?”

“Seeing him was such a shock. I realize I was still kind of stuck in limbo, no matter what I've told myself all this time." After a few seconds I whispered, "I've allowed him to steal so much from me."

"I know, but you've been a real trooper. You had my back during all my low times, even while you were hurting."

Zane's gurgling interrupted her words and brought a smile to my lips. I wriggled him in my arms, then hugged him. "He's growing so much every day."

"Yep, and has a mind of his own. I've noticed, for example, that he prefers being in our bed instead of his own."

"What does Doug think about having his space taken over by a six-month-old gangster?"

"He growls, but he's just a big old teddy bear where Zane is concerned."

"Mmmm. A baby does that to you, no matter how tough you think you are." That brought me back to the fact that the man I thought I'd spend my life with had ditched me over a baby. The pain of it swelled in my throat and I had the hardest time getting words past the sudden wash of emotions.

Zane yammered at me, and I encouraged him with nonsense talk. Khalila's marriage and Zane's birth had given Khalila new life. Meanwhile, I'd been playing house for extended periods with men who grew serious, while I had no intention of settling with them. Each time I cut ties, Khalila told me I was only harming myself. She had been lucky to find love after losing her family to death and divorce. Despite what she said, I knew exactly what I was doing. Why get attached when men could be so fickle?

Her romance with Doug had brought Roger into my life. Now that he wanted commitment from me, I didn't know whether I was coming or going. One thing was sure, it was time I started living but I needed to be out of the same environment as Marcus. I didn't want him contacting me and I needed to get my mind sorted out before I made any life-changing decisions. I turned Zane so he faced Khalila.

"I think I'm going to fly home to Jamaica and spend some quality time by myself. I'm a free agent for now, so I'll come back in a few weeks after I've decided where I'm going next."

We exchanged a grin and I set Zane on his bottom.

"Do whatever you have to and if you need to talk, I'm a phone call away. Just let me know when you're coming and we'll pick you up at the airport." She opened her arms to Zane, who crawled toward her. "When you arrive, I'll want a detailed outline of your plans."

I pulled back, as if outraged. "You don't think I'm about to hatch a plot to dismember Marcus, do you?"

"If anybody else asked me that question, I'd say no. With you, I can't be sure."

Her voice carried an edge that told me she was only half joking.

"Rest assured," I said, waving one hand. "Marcus isn't worth the time."

When Zane was snug in her arms, Khalila warned, "I hope you remember that if you run into each other again."

* * *

I'd been flying around like a bat out of hell since I woke this morning. Sunday was a relaxed affair with Khalila and me taking Zane to the park for an outing. She cautioned me about getting too deep inside my head. Because she'd suffered with depression, Khalila understood all too well where that could lead.

Today, she was alone with Zane, and Doug had gone to a meeting, so I called a cab to take me to the airport. The driver made up the time I lost waking late, and I was relieved to finally sit in the American Airlines bay and wait for my flight to be called. I'd avoided thinking about both Roger and Marcus this morning, but my brain was circling back to that restaurant scene.

Roger texted me earlier to tell me I couldn't avoid him forever. I'd been good so far between Saturday and Sunday, missing his call while in the shower and ignoring his messages to get in touch with him. I didn't know why he was being so persistent since I told him I'd be in touch. He clearly didn't think I'd live up to my word.

On the way to the airport, I missed another call from him but listened to the message. The resignation in his tone was clear when he said he'd see me in a couple of days. He'd probably be in California on business, he said, but would stay in touch.

I got out a *National Geographic* magazine I'd borrowed from Khalila and flipped through it until I came to a feature on Alaska and wild bears. How wonderful it would be to just pick up and go for a visit. As I scanned the pictures, it occurred to me that there was nothing preventing me from doing exactly that. It would take some planning, but was doable.

Money wasn't a reason not to go and time away would mean having the space to cleanse my palate of the man I'd escaped and the man who wanted to tie me down. My insides turned upside down every time I thought about what a relationship with Roger might look like and whether the day would come when he'd have a reason to reject me and walk out of my life. He wasn't flighty, but my trust in men was non-existent.

Hearing Roger's name yanked me back into the airport. The same airline I was flying with was calling him for a flight destined to the Bahamas. My mind said it couldn't be him because he was supposed to be headed to California, but something inside knew it was likely to be my Roger.

I backtracked to my conversations with both him and Douglas and their inability to give me a satisfactory explanation as to why he was always MIA at critical times. While we weren't at the place where I felt I could ask unlimited questions, no matter how brash I was at times, Roger had made up his mind about me. If that didn't give me the right to ask questions, I didn't know what did.

Each time a man of Roger's height and skin color walked by, my attention strayed from the magazine. It wasn't long before Roger came striding up the corridor with a small duffle in one hand. My heart raced at the sight of him in jeans and a dark polo as his long legs propelled him swiftly through the terminal. The neatly trimmed beard and dark glasses gave him an intense and mysterious air. I tamped down the adrenaline flowing through my veins and waited until he was abreast of where I sat before calling his name.

Roger's head swiveled toward me and his eyes widened. "Corinne."

I rose from my seat and stood in his path. "Seems California got a new name."

He winced and one of his eyes narrowed. The announcer called his name again along with the flight number and destination, and he looked over my shoulder. His gaze came back to me and he switched the bag to his other hand. "There's a good explanation for this."

"I should hope so."

"But I can't give it to you now."

"I didn't expect you would." I stepped away from him. "You need time to concoct something believable."

His eyes closed, then he refocused on me. "I'd never lie to you, Corinne."

A fake smile crossed my lips. "But you just did."

He hung his head, then drew one hand across the back of his neck. "Forgive me." Tipping his head to one side, he asked, "Where are you going? When did you plan to tell me you were leaving?"

"Back to Jamaica."

His lips quirked and he gave me a rueful smile. "I suppose you would have told me at some point, huh?"

"Maybe."

A last call for Roger interrupted our conversation.

He cupped my cheek and stepped in closer.

Everything inside told me not to allow him to touch me, but my heart didn't listen.

Roger laid his lips over mine and without my permission, my mouth opened for his kiss. Eyes closed, I savored our connection as his tongue caressed mine and reminded me of all the reasons I was into him despite what my mind was telling me. My hands rested at his waist as our kiss deepened and I forgot where we stood.

When he raised his head, a sigh passed Roger's lips. He dropped another kiss at the corner of my mouth. "I gotta go. We'll talk when I catch up with you."

I didn't say yes or no, but watched him walk away.

What on earth was Roger involved in that he couldn't share with me now?

ten

THE DESIRE TO kill Roger was becoming old. I was in the middle of getting ready when the doorbell rang and shortly afterward Khalila came upstairs with a showy floral arrangement. At the sight of it, I knew Roger had failed to appear for our date and the tulips and Godiva chocolate were supposed to pacify me for his absence.

"I'm sure he has a good reason for not coming." Khalila cleared a space on the dresser and set the vase on the mahogany surface.

"Well, he'd better be dead since that's the only excuse I'm accepting for him not showing up."

She swallowed laughter, then said, "Doug agrees that his timing is terrible, but I'm certain—"

"You're certain of a lot of facts about a man who's extremely unreliable, aren't you?"

My glare would have deterred anyone else, but not Khalila. She sat on the bed and looked at me in the mirror. "I wouldn't call him that exactly. Roger just moves around a lot."

I faced her and folded my arms. "Kind of like a rolling stone, you mean?"

"I wouldn't say that either." She shrugged, then smiled when she looked at the yellow tulips. "It's the nature of his business."

Although I didn't care to say it, I knew what Roger meant by sending the arrangement. Yellow was supposedly the color of forgiveness. He knew I favored anything in peach, so I received his message loud and clear. Whether I planned to forgive him was another matter. One thing was certain, I'd had enough of his tomfoolery.

Biting back a sigh, I sat next to Khalila. "I'm the most impatient person I know, so his disappearing acts are beginning to wear on my nerves."

"I don't agree with that." Khalila moved her head from side to side. "You've been extremely tolerant with me, especially while I was going through my issues."

"First of all, I owe it to you. That's what friends do. Secondly, I could afford to be patient. You suffered a big loss. Losing a child is no joke. *Thirdly*, Roger is a forty-one-year-old man. What adults do is talk about how their actions impact other people in their lives. Roger clearly has different views." I put a hand to the gold choker at my throat. "I'm not up for any foolishness, least of all with people who should know better."

Rising from the bed, I pulled off the sleeveless black dress and stepped out of my heels. Sitting in Doug and Khalila's house wouldn't give me any of the answers I needed. Finding Roger would.

Khalila watched as I drew on a pair of jeans and a T-shirt. While I pulled on my sneakers, I said, "I need your car keys."

"Where are you going?"

On my way back from the dresser, I slipped my cell into my jeans pocket. "To find Roger."

She eyed me as if I'd lost my mind. "Are you sure you want to do this?"

"I've never been more certain of anything. Are you giving me those keys, or not?"

"Maybe Doug could—"

"Lila, this has nothing to do with Doug. Be thankful you got the pick of Ms. Hyacinth's litter."

She chuckled and rewound the hair that escaped from the bun on top of her head. "If you want to describe two as a litter..."

Tugging her arm, I said, "Come on."

Before opening the door, I stopped and faced her. "Don't tell Doug where I've gone."

Khalila frowned. "And what exactly am I going to say if he asks where you went since he was sitting in the living room when the flowers came?"

"Tell him I'm a grown woman and he doesn't need to worry about me."

She stood in front of me and rested a hand on my shoulder. "Promise me something."

"As long as it's doable."

Concern filled her eyes and she touched my cheek. "Don't do anything you'll regret."

"I'll certainly try but I can't say how successful I'll be."

Khalila grimaced and stepped aside. "Call me when you find him."

"What are you going to do, put on your Superwoman cape and rush in to save him?"

"No, but I can talk you out of doing something stupid."

Despite my annoyance, I chuckled. "Don't worry, I'm not so hung up on Roger that I'd do anything crazy."

"Which doesn't explain why you're rushing out of here like a frog with salt on its back searching for the nearest body of water." Her expression and attitude were sour, but neither fazed me.

Turning the doorknob, I laughed. "By the way, I object to being compared to a frog."

"And *I* object to what you're doing, but you're still about to do your own thing."

With a breezy wave I sang, “Every minute of the day.”

We walked down the stairs and I was thankful Doug wasn’t sitting in the living room. While he wouldn’t question my movements, if Khalila had a mind to ask him to intervene, chances were I’d listen to him and change my mind about leaving the house. Like his brother, Doug could be persuasive, plus his arguments were always concise and sensible. Right now, I didn’t want to see reason.

When we stood at the front door, Khalila put her keys in my hand. “Don’t do anything you’ll have to apologize for.”

Gently, I squeezed her hand, lying through my teeth. “I won’t.”

Behind the wheel of Khalila’s Tesla, I asked myself if I was prepared for anything I might find when I tracked Roger down. I inhaled deeply and told myself I was ready. That man had contacted me every day, one way or another, in the two weeks since I left Miami. I didn’t always answer his calls.

Sometimes, we texted. Other times, we talked by WhatsApp. In that fourteen-day stretch, I limited our conversations to five times because Roger was enough to throw my thought process off kilter, and I didn’t need any distractions. Now that I was back after a period of reflection, contemplating my past and possible future, I wasn’t willing to accept that Roger would “no show” minus a good reason.

Without a doubt, he’d be shocked to see me. In the early days, I thought Roger always stayed at a hotel, but each time we met outside of the States, his luggage tag carried a Miami address. I made it my business to check, and though my actions made me feel like a stalker, I memorized the address just in case.

I’d never questioned him about his movements whenever we were in America at the same time, except for when we met at the airport the day I left Miami. Nor had we ever discussed where he stayed when he wasn’t in a hotel room or at Doug’s house.

Whether or not he was happy to see me wasn’t the point. He’d failed to show up once too often and I wasn’t prepared to give him any more of my time if he couldn’t be honest about the reason for his dodgy behavior.

I had a good sense of direction and would find where his apartment was located in the city. My only fear was that, when I found him, Roger might also demand answers from me about the direction of our relationship.

eleven

THE DOORBELL JERKED me awake and I sat up, groaning. My stomach muscles reminded me of their tender state when I tried to get up. Who would dare to disturb me this evening? I never had visitors here except Neil and nobody we allowed to stay at the apartment ever returned.

I'd canceled my date with Corinne because there was no way I could turn up looking and feeling like I'd been worked over by a heavyweight boxer. She would be mad as hell, but I didn't have a choice.

Whoever was at the door leaned on the button again, flooding the apartment with more unwanted noise.

I removed Bessie from under my pillow, then hobbled to the door and yelled, "Who is it?"

The visitor chose not to answer.

The job, plus some of the incidents I'd seen in my time, made me superstitious. For that reason, I never put my face up against any peephole. I didn't fancy being shot in the eye. I held the gun against my sweat bottom and yanked the door open. "Who do you ..."

My annoyance slipped away as I met Corinne's eyes. "What are you doing here? How did you find me?"

The shock I felt was reflected on her face. Frown lines appeared across Corinne's forehead, and she narrowed her eyes. "You look like you were on *Monday Night Raw*."

A smile lifted one corner of my mouth, but disappeared when my split lip stung.

Corinne studied me for another moment before she stepped forward, which forced me to retreat into the apartment. I caught the glimmer of sympathy in her eyes, and my admiration for her climbed by several notches. She hadn't acted like a drama queen over my appearance—and I was a sight—but she had questions.

Arms folded, she said, "It's obvious why you skipped out on me."

She shut the door behind her and leaned against it, scanning me from head to bare feet. Aside from a slight lift of the eyebrows at the sight of my hand still hidden behind one leg, her expression didn't change. Corinne walked past me, forcing me to follow her into the living area. She dropped her purse on the coffee table and focused on me. "How long have we known each other?"

That was the last question I expected her to ask. "Close to two years, give or take."

"And have I done anything to make you think I don't have a solid head on my body?"

"No." I sat on the edge of one of the small sofas, stifling a moan.

As Corinne's face contracted with concern, I slid the gun into the space beside the cushion. Her gaze followed the movement of my hand, but she didn't remark on it. Instead, she sat on the other deep-blue sofa and crossed her legs. "On that basis, don't you think you can tell me why you keep disrupting our dates...before I give up on you totally?"

I caught myself frowning. "You'd do that because I disappointed you a few times?"

She lowered her chin and arched one brow. "A few times?"

Rubbing the back of my head, I said, "Work has been intense these past few months, I admit..."

A grin lit Corinne's face, which I didn't expect. "You're forgetting the part about it being dangerous."

I bit back a smile. "If you say so."

"What else would have you looking like you had a run-in with someone's fist?"

Sighing, I tipped my head back. How would I explain why I was in this condition?

Corinne rose and stood in front of me. She studied my face before touching me. When she did, her fingers skimmed my forehead, which was turning a deep shade of purple. Her exploration of my eye had me pulling back.

"Tender, huh?"

Nodding, I met her gaze.

She lifted my chin, her attention focused on my cheek, then my lips. She touched hers to mine, then murmured. "You expect me to be open with you, yet you're hiding your business from me."

"I would have upset you if I turned up looking like this."

"Trust me, I'm more upset that you didn't show." She pointed to my face. "These look like you've cleaned them up."

I nodded again. "Yeah, I'll be fine."

Arms folded she stepped back, giving me a view of her close-fitting T-shirt and skinny jeans. "So what happened?"

The second she stepped into the apartment, we'd been working toward this moment but I was stumped. I'd dealt with people at all levels of society and held my own—clergymen and women, company executives, government ministers, world leaders, and ordinary folks—yet this woman had the power to reduce me to being without words to express myself.

"I did business with someone a couple of weeks ago and the deal didn't work out as planned. His associates didn't agree with—"

Corinne's upraised hand halted my explanation. "That's weak. If you can't tell me the truth, there's no point in wasting your words."

I opened my mouth to defend my lies, but she cut me off. "Have you eaten?"

"Not lately."

She moved toward the kitchen. "D'you have anything edible here? I'm starving."

Her change of direction would have startled someone else, but not me. I understood Corinne better than she thought. Later, when I wasn't expecting it, she'd circle back to this conversation. I would be ready because the less she knew, the more peace of mind she'd have.

Corinne opened the refrigerator and looked at me over her shoulder. "How on earth can anyone survive on butter, water, and salad dressing?"

"I guess we have to order in." With my chin, I pointed toward the small desk against one wall. "There's a menu card there for a Chinese restaurant that's close by. We can order from them. I already know what I want."

She got out the menu card and sat opposite me. While she ran down the list of dishes, I watched her. She was as different from Rosalie as summer from winter. Maybe that's why she appealed to me so much. Where my wife had been good natured and dependent on me, Corinne could be ornery and was as tough as a coconut shell when necessary.

Although she barely gave me glimpses of the tender parts of her character, she had a caring side. It was evident in the fact that she came to seek me out, just to be certain I was alive and well. Her actions said way more than Corinne ever had with her mouth. It occurred to me that she and Khalila were such good friends because they balanced each other.

Corinne laid the menu card in her lap and picked up the cordless phone. "You look like you've made a million-dollar discovery."

"I think I just did."

She dialed and put the phone to her ear. "Care to share?"

"When you're done," I said, knowing I was about to spin the ball back into Corinne's court in a way she wouldn't like.

A couple of minutes later, she ended the call and returned the menu card to the drawer. She sat on the sofa and curled her legs sideways with her eyes laser focused on me. "So what brilliant bit of knowledge came to you just now?"

"Despite how you act, you just proved you're a softie."

She chuckled, then said, "You think because I came over here to find you, that constitutes me being soft?"

"I didn't say you were spineless. What I meant is that you care for me."

"That's a given." She waved one hand. "In any case, I came for selfish reasons. I was tired of you standing me up. I'm here to demand an explanation. Should have known pride had something to do with you not showing up."

"I beg your pardon?"

"Don't get your boxers all twisted." She chuckled. "I just mean your pride wouldn't allow you to be seen in public all banged up."

"Call it what you will, Corinne, but I was thinking about you when I decided not to show for our date." Moving slowly, I exchanged my seat for the large sofa and beckoned to her. "Come closer."

She rearranged herself and settled next to me. I slid an arm around her, wincing when her weight rested against my ribs.

Corinne pulled away to look me in the eyes. "Are you sure you're okay, Roger?"

"I'm fine." With the remote, I switched on the television. "Let's watch something until the food gets here."

Corinne kissed my jaw. "Conversation getting too intense for you?"

"Not likely. In case you don't know, I've dealt with much tougher folks than you."

"You have no idea how persistent I can be."

"And you don't know—"

The doorbell interrupted me and when I attempted to get up, Corinne held me back with one hand to my chest. "Stay. I'll get it. That was quick though."

"I need to get my wallet," I said.

"Let's worry about that later. My purse is closer."

We shared a quiet battle of wills as we stared at each other. Corinne wasn't about to back down, so I raised both hands. "Fine, we'll do it your way."

She got up and kissed my forehead. "I like it when you recognize that you don't have to control everything."

The doorbell sounded again.

"Coming," Corinne said, opening her purse. "No need to wear out the buzzer."

Her feistiness brought another smile. The qualities I appreciated most about Corinne were her sassiness and independence. She was woman enough to do for herself and made me laugh while getting the job done. I could easily see myself falling deeper under her spell. If only she'd let me behind the wall she'd built to protect her emotions.

Maybe the only way to get her to open up was to tell her the truth, like she'd asked me to do so many times. My secrecy was doing more damage than good, and if I wanted to keep Corinne, I didn't have any other choice than to tell her what she wanted to know. The more I thought about being honest with her, the better I felt. We had the entire evening to talk, so I'd come clean after we ate.

All of a sudden, my scalp prickled, a bad sign.

"Corinne?"

A scream and a thud had me standing in a second.

twelve

THE DOOR SLAMMED and two men rushed into the living room, their guns pointed at me.

Aside from a tic around my eye, and my heart banging against my ribs, I didn't move.

"Where is he?" the tall, light-skinned goon in front of me snarled through the head tie covering his face.

I raised both brows and asked, "Who?"

"Your partner," he spat.

"Jace." The other guy, a foot shorter with a coal-black complexion, spoke at the same time.

The intruders looked at each other, which gave me the space I needed.

"What did you do to her?"

"Shut up, we're asking the questions." The taller man raised the gun to eye level.

Their jumpiness, the blingy branded caps, and the head ties covering the bottom half of their faces, confirmed these boys were initiates. Their youthfulness was clear in the way they spoke and carried themselves. I also guessed their handler figured I'd be easy pickings. These two were dangerous, since they had something to prove to whoever sent them.

Keeping my pitch even, I asked, “Where is the woman who answered the door?”

Amusement lit the taller one’s eyes. “Don’t worry about her, she’s out cold for now.”

The shorter teen laughed. “Yeah, she’ll be fine.”

Fury burned in my chest, and I wanted to pummel the shit out of the two of them, but that would be challenging with my sore ribs and the agony at the base of my spine from being kicked repeatedly. I was outgunned, but I certainly had more brain power than the two of them together.

“So, you’ve assaulted a woman and forced your way into my home. For what purpose?”

“We told you. Now where is he?”

“You have to give me a name, otherwise I can’t help you.” Irritation colored my voice while I pretended not to know who they wanted. While they were here interrogating me, Corinne was out front unconscious. The thought of her lying there, hurt, terrorized me.

“Jace.”

“The man who came with you.”

I stifled my impatience, but didn’t shift other than to spread my feet. I waved to encompass the room. “As you can see, he’s not here.”

Neither of them moved to do a search, so I continued, “The woman who answered the door is the only other person here, except me. So...”

The light-skinned gunman took two steps and kicked my foot sideways. “You think you’re funny, huh?”

I shook my head and righted myself. “My *partner* isn’t here, as you can see.”

Still in my face, the hoodlum stabbed me with a glare and waved his gun. “Dre, check the bedrooms and bathrooms.”

The shorter teenager winced, then walked away to do the search.

I didn't know whether to be amused or upset. Whoever heard of gang members calling names during a home invasion? These two clowns were rank amateurs aiming to get themselves locked up. They were wasting my time while my woman might be in need of medical assistance. I swallowed hard because I still didn't know what they had done to her. This situation needed to end fast.

With the gun trained on me and the tall one watching me like a hawk hunting prey, I had to wait for an opportunity when he lowered his guard.

Or I could make one, which I much preferred.

As if he heard my thoughts, he backed up until he stood square in the area where the living room met the passage to the front door.

I pointed toward the front door and shuffled my feet to ease the pain in my back. "Listen, can I go check on her?"

"Old man, shut up. I said she'd be okay." He threw a glance over his shoulder and settled cold eyes on me. "I don't know what you can do in your condition anyway."

His casual comment told me he was fully aware of the beating I'd taken yesterday. I couldn't remember him being there, but who knew? I was busy trying to keep the bastards who attacked me from kicking my teeth down my throat.

His gaze shifted to where his companion had gone, then the doorbell sounded and startled him. That's when the room erupted.

Corinne appeared from the corridor and raced toward him.

In the time it took for me to yell her name, she swung the cast-iron floor lamp at him and he crumpled to the floor.

Dre rushed back into the living room when a bang echoed through the area. All three of us crouched instinctively. Someone else had broken into the apartment.

I recovered first and hobbled toward Corinne, trying to get a glimpse down the passage.

Dre swung the gun wildly, and I was sure he'd drop Corinne in a minute. His hand shook and his finger jerked against the trigger.

As I launched myself at Corinne, Neil sailed into the room, gun in hand.

Another bang made the furniture shudder.

As I landed on top of Corinne, Dre howled. Every part of my body hurt, but I stayed in position while she flailed to get me off her.

"Keep still." I winced as she poked me in the ribs.

She opened her mouth to protest, then whimpered when she focused over my shoulder.

A familiar pair of black leather boots came into view. Relief flooded through me, and I turned my head to meet Corinne's terrified gaze. "It's okay. He's on our side."

I rolled over and Neil put out a hand.

Using his grip as leverage, I slowly stood. "Thanks, man."

In turn, I helped Corinne get back on her feet.

She threw a doubtful look in Neil's direction and drew closer to me. I put an arm around her and pulled her forward. "Neil meet Corinne. Corinne, Neil."

A series of moans echoed through the apartment. "Help me. I need help."

"Don't worry about him," Neil said. "I'll call an ambulance."

He disappeared into one of the bedrooms and on his return, he stood over the teenager he shot. After yanking the covering off the boy's face, Neil said, "I need to know why you and your friend found it necessary to break into this apartment." He walked to where the other young man lay and prodded him with one foot. He didn't move.

Neil threw me a length of cord, with which I secured the unconscious teen's wrists. I tugged the fabric down, uncovering his face. Just as I thought, these two were mere kids.

"I'm not a patient man." Neil words opposed his calm demeanor. "I need answers."

When he turned the gun back on Dre, I butted in. "You'd better talk and save yourself the trouble of being dead when the police get here."

The boy on the floor blubbered and clutched his bleeding shoulder as tears sprang to his eyes.

Corinne gasped and was about to protest when I gripped her arm and threw her a stern look I hoped she could interpret. As she stared into my eyes, she drew a deep breath. She decided to trust me.

Neil and I had played these roles a few times over the years. He was a master at intimidation tactics and his mentorship of young adults helped him read them in these situations.

Neil aimed at the gunman's head.

He cowered into a fetal position. "I'll tell you. Please don't kill me."

Cool as a winter's day, Neil issued an instruction. "Get up."

Dre scrambled to his feet, grunting and nursing his shoulder as blood poured through his fingers.

"How do I know you'll be telling me the truth?" Neil asked.

"You're holding a gun on me, man." Dre's head whipped back and forth as he panicked again. "I wouldn't tell no lies."

Neil walked away and returned, but didn't look convinced. "Who sent you?"

Dre sobbed. "You're going to make him hurt me."

"Well, you better pick your poison. Either him or me." A scowl twisted Neil's face. "And right now, you're wearing out my patience."

"Please. Don't do this." Dre cowered as liquid flowed down his legs and darkened his jeans. He wiped his nose with the back of his hand and continued begging.

Beside me, Corinne gripped my arm as if unsure that Neil wouldn't harm Dre.

The wailing of sirens rivaled the sound of Neil cocking his Taurus G3.

thirteen

"NOTHING COULD HAVE PREPARED me for being hit with a stun gun."

"I agree," Khalila said, then sipped coffee. Her eyes danced over the rim of the cup before she lowered it to the table.

"What is it?" I asked, knowing she was holding something back.

Khalila poked out her lips before her smile came through. "Don't take this the wrong way, but I told you so."

"How can you even say that? If I wasn't as healthy as a horse, that taser could have put me in the morgue."

Laying a hand over mine, Khalila said, "I'm sorry, that was insensitive."

"You think?" I snorted, but all she did was hide a grin.

"Come on, though," Her eyes flashed with amusement. "I did tell you not to do anything stupid."

"You clearly didn't hear when I said that man just jabbed me in the chest. I didn't get a chance to do anything."

"The point I'm making is that if you hadn't gone over *there*, you'd have been *here*, safe with me."

"You don't know how to comfort the fallen, do you?"

Khalila almost fell over laughing. When she stopped, her gaze slid toward the doorway. "Did you and Roger make any progress?"

"I think we understand each other a little better."

She beamed at me. "That's good."

I spun the mug in my hand as I tried to wrap my mind around what I was feeling. The danger we'd been in yesterday from those two idiots gave me pause to think about life and how tenuous it was. My experience hadn't included my life flashing before my eyes or anything like that, since being zapped with what amounted to fifty thousand volts of electricity didn't leave any time for thinking.

My ordeal hadn't ended there. The delivery guy came and before I could pay him, he caught sight of Neil and his gun and ran back down the corridor with the food. Dre, the guy Neil had threatened, melted into a helpless puddle on the floor, clutching one of his ears.

Neil, against Roger's advice, had discharged the weapon a second time.

Dre had peed on himself, then divulged more than Neil and Roger wanted to know. His friend, who we later found out was named Calvin, regained consciousness at that point.

While that was going on, I wondered if Neil was playing with a full deck. He didn't strike me as unbalanced, but I had my doubts he wouldn't shoot Dre again. Then I remembered what his friend did to me and kept my mouth shut. As long as Neil didn't do him irreparable harm, I'd be okay.

When the police came, they took eons to write our statements and conduct their due diligence. By the time everybody left, I was extra famished and we ordered more food.

The evening ended with me staying the night with Roger. Wrapped in his arms, inhaling his masculine scent, made me admit I didn't want to be anywhere else. I believed we'd connected on a deep level, but neither of us had acknowledged that fact. Maybe we were both afraid to admit our need for each other out loud.

As he ran the raspy tips of his fingers over my skin and nuzzled my neck, I admitted that I'd never felt more at home with anyone.

We had no need for words, and though we couldn't make love because of the pain Roger wouldn't admit was far worse than he let on, I didn't feel deprived. Being in his arms was enough.

Up to now, I still didn't comprehend what had changed his mind about the direction of our relationship, and I hoped he wouldn't dig too deeply into how Marcus and I were connected. I wasn't ready to disclose that part of my history. I didn't need Roger's pity. I wanted his love.

My thoughts startled me and my gaze shot to Khalila, who was watching me. She waved a finger in front of my face. "Something happened there a while ago. As if you just discovered an amazing fact."

"Not at all." I kept my response low key because I didn't want her to read more into my reaction.

Only in the last few months had Khalila stopped harassing me about my love life. She believed I needed someone to love, outside of the temporary liaisons I had over the years.

I frowned into my cup, wondering why I'd never thought about Roger as an enduring part of my life before now. After Marcus, I didn't allow myself to think about setting down permanent digs.

Khalila squeezed my hand and gave me a half-smile. "You should know better than what you're doing. You can fool anybody else, but not me."

Doug walked into the kitchen with Zane in his arms. "I hope I'm not interrupting anything."

"No, you're good," I said, relieved to see him.

I wasn't afraid of sharing my thoughts with Khalila, but I preferred to talk through my challenges with her *after* I dealt with them myself.

"You're going to see Roger today?"

"Later this afternoon."

Doug seated Zane in Khalila's lap. "I've arranged for a doctor to see him since he insists on being stubborn."

"Good, because he refuses to listen to me."

After noticing that his gingerly movements had worsened last night, I asked Roger if he didn't think he needed a doctor. He waved away my concern. "I've been in much worse condition. I'll be fine," were his exact words.

Despite his protests, the man was exhausted, and I was sure he was about to share important information with me last night moments before he fell asleep. Roger was an even bigger mystery now, and until I knew exactly what he was involved in, I'd be pumping the brakes on our relationship.

That detail, I wouldn't share with Khalila. She was too much of a romantic to see that Roger's secrecy meant he was involved in shady business, or he didn't trust me. Or both.

* * *

I poked my head out of the kitchen in Roger's apartment. "D'you want vegetables with your curried goat or rice?"

"Both," he answered from the living room, where he sat in front of the television watching a program on BBC.

"Okay. Be there in a minute."

A search of the cupboards for dishes and cutlery helped me prepare his dinner that I brought over from Khalila's house.

Doug had done one better than he said this morning. He asked the doctor, a friend of his, to meet us at Roger's place. Both of them left a half-hour ago after Dr. Granger examined Roger and gave him medication, plus a prescription which Doug agreed to fill. The doctor recommended the use of an ice pack for his back and chest. He also told Roger to rest. Then he and Doug left us alone.

Despite Roger's Secret Squirrel behavior that worked my last nerve, I couldn't be anywhere but with him. I hadn't slept much last night, but in racking my brain, it occurred to me that if I wanted a future with Roger, I'd have to force his hand. Either he was going to tell me what I needed to know or be prepared to have me walk out of his life.

I let him enjoy his meal, then cleaned up and returned to sit next to him on the sofa.

"That was good," he said, beckoning me closer.

My smile was indulgent, but I didn't move. "It's one of Khalila's specialties. Girlfriend can cook."

"That's for sure." He studied me for a moment, then said, "I get the feeling you have something up your sleeve."

I leaned away from him as though surprised. "You're smarter than you look."

He chuckled, then winced and touched the side of his mouth. The deep timbre of his voice was always pleasant to my ear and his laughter, inviting. Sprawled across from me in sweat bottoms and a T-shirt, he exuded sexiness. Even with the bruises darkening his skin, he appealed to me. I wanted to run my hand over the stubble on his cheek and kiss him until he was breathless, but his words derailed my thoughts.

"So, what is it you want to say to me that has you looking so thoughtful?"

"I want to talk about us. This half-baked romance between you and me."

His smile faded and he placed a hand on his stomach. "Half-baked? I'm insulted. Especially since I'm the one who's been chasing you all this time."

"You're right about that, but your approach is all kinds of wrong."

He sat up and laced his fingers together. "What on earth d'you mean?"

I changed position so I sat facing him with my legs curled on the seat and my toes peeking out from under my dress. "*You know*, Roger. A year ago, it didn't bother me when you'd call me from different places, because I thought you were making business deals. Lately, that doesn't seem to be the case."

He tried to interrupt, but I laid a hand on his leg to keep him quiet.

"It doesn't look good on you to keep disappearing when we're supposed to spend time together. In fact, I'm starting to think you're a drug dealer or in some other kind of unsavory business."

Roger's wide eyes and the confusion that drew his eyebrows together a moment later was almost comical, but I wasn't laughing. The strong British accent from the television anchor filled the air between us as I waited for him to say something. Roger ran a hand over the back of his head and took a deep breath. "Trust me, Corinne. That's the furthest thing from what I do."

With my eyebrows raised, I asked, "Trust you, Roger? You're asking too much. I'm at the point where your shenanigans are getting the better of me."

I raised both hands in the air with my palms facing him. "I've loved the adventure of meeting up with you in different cities, but you're wearing me out. Frankly, you're making me think that a man with a steady job who's in one place is a better proposition than continuing this hit-and-miss arrangement with you."

"Corinne—"

"Don't 'Corinne' me." I wrapped my arms around my legs and met his gaze. "I'm tired, Roger. Tired of not knowing which way is up with you. Tired of not being sure you'll show when we have a date. And even more tired of the uncertainty that we're on the same page. Yet, you claim you want to go deeper with me."

"I do, Corinne. Never doubt for a second that I want you." He touched my skin, letting his fingers run up and down my arm. "The trouble is, I've grown used to being on my own and not having to account to anyone. Trust me when I say—"

I ignored the tingling where Roger still had contact with my skin. "That's where we have a problem. You keep asking me to trust you, but I can only do that when you've earned that right. Fact is, you haven't given me a reason to believe you want us, other than your words."

He sighed and withdrew his hand. "What can I do to prove that I want you? That I want us?"

Arms folded, I said, “For starters, you can tell me what it is that competes with our time together.”

Roger stared at the television and didn’t respond. His facial expression ran the gamut from doubt to uneasiness to resignation. He looked at me and pulled in a deep breath. On the exhale, he closed his eyes. “Neil and I have a business together. We rescue people in dangerous situations. This can be anywhere and these assignments crop up at any time.”

I took a moment to digest his words. His explanation sounded incredible because it was unexpected. Yet, it made perfect sense when I thought about his incessant traveling. His matter-of-fact words brought relief and were also anticlimactic. In another few seconds, I was annoyed because of his unnecessary cloak-and-dagger attitude.

“That’s your secret? You’re helping people and you act as if you’re doing something illegal?”

“I didn’t want you to worry about me when we weren’t together.” He turned his head toward me. “What I do is taxing on a relationship. Neil’s ex-wife can attest to that.”

I picked up one of his hands and frowned at it. After his confession, I now understood why I’d never equated his rough fingertips with the business of coffee and spices. The trinkets he’d given me each time he went on a trip were meant to pacify me, but the thought of where he’d been and his activities made my heart lose its normal rhythm. “So when were you planning to tell me about this side of your life?”

“I intended to, but I wanted us to enjoy the moments we spend together, so this conversation has gone on the back burner more than once.” He rubbed his head with both hands. “I should have told you sooner. I’m sorry.”

“You’re right about that.” I rested against the back of the seat, still thinking about his revelation. If I had followed my mind and walked away without asking any questions, I’d have followed the pattern I’d lived for too long. Even so, I wasn’t about to go all in with

Roger. He still had lots of ground to cover before he regained my confidence.

His voice jolted me back to the present. “Since we’re clearing the air, can I ask you a couple of questions?”

My breath stuttered because I was certain of one question he’d ask. It would be unfair of me to refuse, so I nodded.

“How d’you feel about Marcus Larmond now? From your reaction to him, I know he hurt you.”

My heart sped up, and I wanted to swipe at the perspiration about to pop out on my forehead. I acted as if I was relaxed when I wanted nothing more than to change the subject. After my gaze wandered to the paintings on the wall and back to Roger, I shrugged. “He’s a mistake I wish I hadn’t made, but I’m over him.”

Roger was laser focused on my face, but I refused to look at him again.

“So, if he wanted back in—”

“He wouldn’t stand a chance,” I quickly cut in with a hard tone. “Can we change the subject? I don’t want to talk about him now.”

Or ever.

Roger threaded his fingers through mine, then shot me a concerned look. “Are you okay?”

My hands had gone ice cold and my stomach was queasy.

I forced a smile and drew closer to him. When I nipped his ear, Roger brushed my jaw with his and let the tip of his tongue tease my skin. Our lips met and I forgot about everything except the spark of desire between us. Several languorous kisses later, I was ready to crawl into Roger’s lap. He eased one arm around me and whispered in my ear. “I want you so bad, split lip, aching back, and all.”

I got to my feet and tugged his hand, happy for the diversion. When he stood, I grinned and kissed the corner of his mouth. “I’m happy to oblige you by doing all of the work this time.”

“Sounds like a plan.” He held me at the waist as he stared into my eyes. “There’s another question I need to ask, but I’ll wait. Just know that we're not yet finished with this conversation. Not by a long shot."

fourteen

AFTER YESTERDAY'S interlude and the slice of heaven I enjoyed with Corinne, Monday morning found me back on the case that was turning out to be way more trouble than Neil and I anticipated.

My best stone face was in play when I said, "There's more to this than you're telling us."

Marcus and Angella glanced at each other, then stared at me over the center table as if they thought I was stupid.

I shifted as if to rise from the seat, which made my back twinge. "There are other things I'd much rather be doing, so stop wasting my time."

"Let's not be hasty," Neil said, in a play to make our clients think I intended to walk out on them. "Let me see if I can break this down."

From the other end of the sofa, he buttonholed the couple. "As Blythe was trying to explain, your son is in deeper than you think."

Angella's eyes were red and watery, as if she'd been crying non-stop since the weekend. She could learn a thing or two from Corinne. She'd been zapped and caught in a situation not of her own making. Plus, she'd been a trooper until the point where she almost intervened in Neil's handling of that wanna-be thug, Dre.

Angella sniffled, then asked, "What do we need to tell you for you to get him back?"

"It's not only a matter of *getting him back*. Jace seems more than happy with the company he's keeping and what he's doing." My gaze shifted between the two of them to underscore the seriousness of the situation. "The point is that your son is into something deeper than you both led me to believe, which resulted..." I pressed a hand to my torso, then pointed toward my face. "...in some bruised ribs and other injuries."

"Which means," Neil added, "that he's perfectly at liberty not to want to help you."

They didn't have to know my injuries weren't as severe as I made them out to be. The bruises on my face would fade by the end of the week. My ribs hadn't been affected much. Although the doctor advised that I should rest to accelerate the healing process, Neil and I had a score to settle with Carey. We'd been on the hunt since earlier in the day. Then Angella called and let us know Jace hadn't been home over the weekend.

We let the silence descend in the room until it stretched to the point where Marcus and Angella could barely keep still. Neil and I sat at ease, as if we had all evening. At this point I should have walked away, but for the fact that the police hadn't been able to find Carey. He'd tracked me down to the apartment, which meant we'd underestimated him. Not to mention we'd gotten careless. His cronies intercepted me on the street, close to the apartment after I'd picked up a few personal care items at a convenience store and was returning on foot.

"Hey, old man."

When I turned my head curbside, a group of thugs surrounded me and attempted to pull me into their vehicle, but my training kicked in. I fought them off, giving as good as I got, with punches and kicks. That hadn't stopped them from raining some serious blows on me. I was back on my feet and in the middle of a roundhouse kick when an older woman came upon us battling it out on the sidewalk and screamed for help.

They jumped into their ride, a black SUV, and hurtled down the street.

After reassuring the old lady I would be okay, I gathered my groceries and hobbled to the apartment.

These guys didn't give up. As long as Carey was somewhere free and clear, Neil and I had to watch our backs. Plus, l didn't want to bring that kind of drama to my brother's house. Or, to Corinne. She'd already walked into my mess by accident. I didn't want her further involved.

At this point, I regretted taking on Marcus's case. I didn't believe in coincidences and it was weird and too convenient that he was connected to Corinne's past. She sounded like she'd gotten over Larmond, but she'd been almost flippant, which was at odds with throwing water in his face.

That wasn't the action of someone who'd gotten over a past lover. I couldn't help feeling that Corinne didn't believe I'd see their relationship for what it was—her making a bad choice in Marcus, which she couldn't have predicted or controlled.

When my gaze settled on him, I said, "Let's talk in the kitchen."

He nodded and got to his feet. His sweater, jeans, and house slippers indicated that he planned to be home for the evening. When we stood face to face in the rectangular space bracketed by a matching chrome stove and refrigerator, I shoved both hands in my pockets and tipped my chin toward the living room. "Here's the deal. I'm not willing to play these games with you and her."

He frowned and folded his arms. "What are you talking about?"

"I'm talking about the fact that you weren't honest with me up front."

"I don't know what you mean," Marcus said, meeting my gaze.

"Don't play with me."

"Look, man," he protested, "I'm doing everything I can to help."

Pointing at him, I said, "I can't prove it, but I think you're yanking me around when it comes to Corinne. I don't know how you knew we were connected, but you used the opportunity when you saw us together to get to her."

I removed both hands from my pockets and mirrored his pose. “You know way more about what that boy's doing than you're admitting. If you want to help him and his mother, you'd better level with me right now. The only reason he’s not in jail with the others is because we chose not to tell them about his involvement.”

For more seconds than I cared to count, Marcus stared at me, then lowered his gaze and sighed. “Truth be told, Angella and I haven't seen much of him since you brought him back. He comes in late at night, leaves early in the morning. We barely see Jace to talk with him. I don’t even know if he was here last night.”

Their domestic affairs concerned me only to the extent that it involved the case. “I notice you’re not saying a thing about Corinne, but I have the memory of an elephant, so we’ll come back to that.”

I wanted to ask how they allowed a teenager to have his way in their house, but I didn't. I’d seen the struggles Doug had with Mo and Kim in the past, and my brother was a strong man.

“D'you mind if I have a look in his room?” I asked.

Marcus shrugged, then shook his head. “Be my guest.”

I followed him down the hallway to a closed door. He pushed it open and darkness met us, thanks to the blackout curtains at the windows. Marcus flipped the switch and I scanned the bedroom, which was a decent size and decorated in several shades of blue. A desk and chair occupied one corner. The bed was positioned under the window and a dresser stood against the other wall.

I pulled out the chair and scanned the leatherette desktop. Either Jace was a neat freak or his mother had come through and tidied up. The latter was most likely the case.

“Can I have a look inside the desk?”

“Go ahead.”

A jumble of paper filled the top drawer. I lifted out a handful and laid them on the desk. After sifting through, I pushed them to one side. From the opposite drawer, I came up with another pile of note-book pages and Post-it notes. Jace was definitely a slob.

I also found a stack of notebooks and several files, which I browsed.

Marcus stepped in closer.

Three cell phones and a list now lay between my hands. Closer examination revealed the phone numbers of persons with Minnesota zip codes.

I didn't need to waste any more brain power wondering what Jace was involved in.

When I looked at Marcus, he stared back in disbelief. “Does this mean what I'm thinking?”

He lowered his voice but it was too late. Neil stood in the doorway, and Angella brushed past him with her gaze riveted on the scattered items.

“What is all that?” She focused on Marcus. “What has Jace been doing in here?”

Neither Marcus nor I answered. Her eyes narrowed as she looked at the list in my hand.

“Is that what I think it is?” One hand went to her neck and her voice grew wobbly. “What on earth is Jace doing with all of those numbers?”

“Angella, for once in your life can you open your eyes? Nobody needs to tell you what this is.”

Marcus turned away, rubbing the back of his neck, while Angella snatched the papers. She covered her mouth with a trembling hand, stifling her sobs.

Marcus walked back across the room and tried to embrace her, but she pushed him away. “Please for heaven's sake,” she pleaded, “tell me what's going on.”

Over Angella's shoulder I met his gaze. I made a slight back and forth movement with my head. Until I knew the extent of Jace's involvement in what appeared to be lottery scamming, I wouldn't put a name to his mother's fears.

Angella deserted Marcus and hurried over to grab my wrists. Her face was ravaged by tears. "Please, you have to do something to help Jace before he ruins his life."

Every time I took cases that involved teenagers, my nieces haunted my thoughts. In today's world, kids needed much more guidance than I did as a child because there were twice as many distractions.

"You have to help us, no matter what it takes," she pleaded.

Neil and I exchanged a glance. His expression said it was my call.

I patted her shoulder. "We'll do what's necessary. But I hope you realize Jace needs more than simply being brought home each time he disappears."

She nodded, then whispered, "Thank you so much." Her eyes watered as she continued, "It doesn't matter what you have to do, or what it costs, please find him."

If I was going to help Marcus and his woman, I had to get some answers for myself, so when we were leaving, I asked him to walk us to the door.

Angella went to her bedroom, and that allowed me to speak to Marcus out of her hearing.

I asked Neil to give us a minute and stood with Marcus by their front door.

"Now is as good a time as any for you to tell me why you chose this point to walk back into Corinne's life. You could have avoided us if you wanted to do so."

He sighed. "It's not like...I just wanted some closure."

"After what you did to her?"

His sheepish expression annoyed me and I wanted to punch him in the face.

"You're going to tell me how you knew I was connected to Corinne." I held up one hand. "I definitely don't want to know why you were stupid enough to think she'd forget how you gutted her by walking out when she needed you."

He looked at the tiles, then raised his head to look over my shoulder. "I saw the two of you together months ago, but didn't approach her then. When we needed help with Jace and you came to see us, I already knew who you were."

He shrugged. "You can't blame a man for trying. The least I could do was apologize to her."

"I'll accept that, but what I won't accept is you trying to contact Corinne again. She doesn't want anything to do with you."

He winced, but I was relentless.

"If I hear you've been near her, I'll come for you myself. Trust me, you won't like the consequences, so stay the hell away from her."

fifteen

ROGER WAS SO USED to being evasive, getting information out of him was like searching for an oasis in a desert. I laid a hand on his leg and squeezed. “So when are you going to tell me why you’re in Jamaica?”

“Isn’t being here with you enough reason?” The back of his hand teased the skin of my cheek. “You’re a fascinating woman.”

“Yes, but at the same time, you’re full of B.S.”

Roger laughed and turned his head out the window of the RAV4 he’d rented.

His laughter was contagious and I joined him. Two weeks had gone by since the incident at the place that wasn’t really his place. Since then, he told me the apartment was where he slept whenever he was in town on business. He hadn’t stayed there when Khalila got married. Nor when he appeared for any other family gathering.

I asked him about that period before we connected as lovers and discovered he stayed elsewhere whenever they used it as temporary housing in a crunch. On those occasions, he rented a hotel room.

We flew into Kingston at my insistence, because I wanted to check on my home. My mother lived happily in her own house with my stepfather, so I didn’t have to worry about her, but we did stop in to see her. The visit with Roger in tow came as a surprise, but she only nodded her approval since I didn't give her time to do much else. Over the years, I'd kept her out of the loop, introducing her to only a few of the men I was seeing.

I'd deliberately scheduled our movements, so we were headed to Montego Bay on the following day. That way, she wouldn't be able to ask questions I couldn't answer. Roger and I had not yet decided how our future would play out, and I wasn't one to make up lies to satisfy anyone, not even my mother.

"What's over there?" Roger asked, tipping his head to the side.

"The Convention Center." Looking at him from the driver's seat, I asked, "Planning something?"

One corner of his mouth lifted. "Let's just say I might have an aim in view."

I wasn't sure about his intentions, but something told me he was on some kind of mission. Roger had more than a passing interest in the landscape.

A week after being beaten up, he brought up the idea of coming to Jamaica for a mini vacation. When I asked how he felt physically, he said he'd be okay to fly. He paid for our tickets, booked us into a villa located in Rose Hall, and here we were.

For the last two days, I'd been lying in the lap of luxury. The villa was situated on an incline and came equipped with every modern convenience, plus a staff of butler, chef, housekeeper, and a small team of cleaners. Aside from reading and absorbing the breath-taking views of the land, and the blues and greens of the Caribbean Sea from the patio, I'd been watching movies in front of the massive television screen and chauffeuring Roger around the bustling city of Montego Bay.

Traffic was always bumper to bumper, but the sights and sounds captured the heartbeat of the island. People peddling their wares from fruit stands and makeshift stalls, the range of shops—from bars to stores selling craft items—and ordinary people going about their business.

I'd never had the chance to view Montego Bay with the eyes of a tourist, so in the cool of the evening, I seized the opportunity to visit the shops on Gloucester Avenue, or The Hip Strip as it was called. Roger was patient and seemed to enjoy what he termed as my treasure hunt. Along the way, I'd bought items for Khalila, Doug, and even a cute onesie for Zane, featuring a baby wearing dreadlocks.

During our drives, I sensed that Roger was looking at our surroundings with more than the eyes of a tourist. He was interested in places that were outside of the ordinary. After he expressed interest in two volatile communities ten minutes apart, I told him, "You may need a special tour guide if you want to go into those places."

"Are you game?" he asked, chuckling.

"I forgot to mention that tour won't include me."

We had a laugh over that, then spent the evening lying on the private beach attached to the property. Now, we lay on a huge blanket, watching the sunset. I snuggled against his chest, thinking it felt right. Despite his wanting us to get closer, I didn't feel threatened by Roger. I also didn't get the sense that he'd blindside me with any questions or requests I couldn't handle. This interlude was supposed to be us rediscovering each other and planning where we went from here. But he was clear that he wouldn't rush me into making a decision.

My hand roamed idly under his tee-shirt and my fingers tangled in his chest hair.

Roger kissed my forehead, then tipped my chin up and met my lips with his. He teased me for several moments until I eased his mouth open. Roger delved into the kiss, leaving me breathless. When we both came up for air, he said, "You've been quieter than normal."

"Been thinking," I said next to his lips.

"What say we put that aside for a bit and enjoy each other?"

"Sounds like a plan." Running my tongue up to his ear, I murmured. "I thought we were going for a swim."

Roger's chuckle rumbled against my skin. "The sea isn't going anywhere. It'll be there when we're done."

His hand closed over the back of my bra and snapped it open, then he flung the scrap of fabric aside. My back arched to meet his lowered head and my eyes closed as he nuzzled the mounds of my breasts. A sigh escaped from me as Roger held me in place, driving me crazy with a rhythmic suckling motion. Meanwhile, his fingers created magic that made me purr with delight.

When I thought I'd dissolve on a tide of lust, he laid a trail of soft kisses down my belly button and lifted my hips to pull down the bottom of my bathing suit. His skillful fingers danced between my thighs and my hips undulated on the blanket. My hands were busy, gently tracing the ridges of his chest muscles while the hairs tickled my skin.

The soothing beat of the water against the shoreline and velvety skies provided a fitting backdrop for our lovemaking. I'd had many adventures with the opposite sex, but making love on the beach at night was a new experience, one I was happy to have Roger share with me.

His foray inside me with his fingers brought me into the present with immediacy as my hips undulated on the fabric. In a swift, fluid move he covered me while whispering in my ear as I wrapped my thighs around him. Our joining was heated and intense, as always. Beyond taking his time to ensure that I was at the same place as he, Roger was relentless.

He tormented me with his hands and mouth, while thrusting inside me until orgasmic shocks spread throughout my entire body. Now, he shifted me so that we lay facing each other. He dipped his head to my breast, and soon had me clinging to him as if he was supplying a life-giving substance. His thigh slid between mine, and he pulled me on top of him, holding me by the hips.

I moaned into his neck as my core clung to him after every stroke. As my thighs trembled, Roger yelled my name and emptied himself inside me. I lay on his chest, panting as if I'd been sprinting. He laid his hand on my back and kissed my hair.

This was part of what kept me tethered to him and our long-distance relationship. He knew how to make me feel as though he'd been saving up to pour into me. Every time we met.

As our heartbeats slowed, Roger turned us and I slid my leg between his muscular thighs.

While the wind rustled the trees above us and the evening deepened into night, I let out a contented sigh. He was half asleep and grumbled at me. Looking at him, I asked, "So, what are we doing tomorrow?"

Laughter was the last thing I expected. He kissed my nose then said, "You don't wait for the sand to shift under your feet, do you?"

"I just wanted to know if you had any special plans."

He yawned and ran one hand over his chest. "I need to check my calendar."

"What kind of answer is that?" I frowned and lifted my head. "Aren't we on vacation?"

"There's some stuff I have to do while I'm here though."

I got up on my elbow and met his eyes in the gloom. "Are you serious?"

He pulled me to his chest. "Don't worry about it. It's not going to take an entire day."

Disappointment lodged in my belly and I sighed. "I kinda knew that there was something. The true reason you wanted to come to Jamaica."

Roger's words were quiet and carried no inflection. "Let's not argue about this. The main reason we're here is for each other. The stuff I might have to do is not that important."

"Really? You lure me here on the premise that we're going to spend time together. Time we've never really had. Then you tell me you had *other stuff* scheduled, and only because I asked."

"It's not that big of a deal, Corinne." He let out a heavy breath.

"Honestly, what I have to do may not take long or intrude on us too much."

"I don't know how you can say that after what went down at the apartment. Seems to me you can't always predict what will happen with your work." The wind was getting chilly, so I sat up and folded both arms around my knees. "I might add that you owe me for saving your ass."

Roger's teeth flashed in a grin and he laid one hand in the middle of my back. "I've thanked you five hundred times for that already."

Shifting toward him, I said, "By the way you're acting, I may have to get out my Superwoman cape again."

He stopped moving, and I waited for him to respond as the waves crested the shore. Roger's voice was strained when he said, "I'm sorry, Corinne. It's hard to teach an old dog new tricks, but I'm trying."

"In the meantime, I'm supposed to look the other way while you continue what you're doing. You can barely even admit that I'm partially right about why we're here."

Roger stroked the skin high on my thigh. "I'm not used to sharing details with anybody but Neil, so I'm going to ask you to be patient with me, okay?"

"Fine, but try to understand that I'm asking questions because I care."

"I get it." Roger raised his head and kissed the middle of my back, sending a shiver up my spine and desire shooting to my core. "And I appreciate your concern more than you know."

"If that's the case, now is a great opportunity to just admit what I've already figured out."

After an interval in which he could have said anything that would have sufficed as an explanation, or confirmation that I was right, Roger decided to remain silent.

When I was tired of waiting, I got to my feet, pulled on my bathing suit, and left him on the beach.

sixteen

WHEN CORINNE WAS annoyed or offended, she was as unmoving as the Rock of Gibraltar. After the sweet lovemaking we shared, she stayed upset and I'd been walking on eggshells all day.

I tried pulling her out by having her take me around town again, but that hadn't worked. One good thing came out of that excursion. I was a bit more familiar with the city of Montego Bay and the surrounding area. Later in the afternoon, she gave me a disbelieving look when I mentioned playing one of the golf courses along the Rose Hall stretch. I figured that had more to do with her doubting that I actually intended to have a game than anything else.

She was right. Half right anyway. I was using the golf outing to lay the groundwork for meeting a local contact.

When we finished lunch, I met Corinne's gaze across the table. "While I'm at the golf course, what are you going to do?"

She made me wait while she chewed a bite of potato pudding. "I'll either stay here or do some shopping."

"Again?"

That slipped out before I could stop it. I knew better but let my mouth run away with me because of the sheer number of gift items she'd already bought.

Corinne pulled her head back. “You have a problem with me spending my own money?”

“No, ma’am. That was me overstepping my boundary.”

One side of her mouth curved. “Right. Since when did you recognize any such thing?”

My laughter eased the tension I’d created since last night. Like Corinne said, I was past the stage where I tiptoed around her. What I wanted to know, I asked. The only place I hadn’t trespassed yet was into her history with Marcus. I wanted to hear it from her but that was unlikely at this present moment.

I fondled her fingers and laced mine through hers. “I only go as far as you let me, as you well know.”

“Are you saying I’m keeping secrets?”

I drank the rest of my water, then said, “Not at all.” Frowning, I asked, “How did we get here?”

She threw me a knowing look, then went in another direction. “So, this round of golf you’re going to play, will you be alone?”

Without missing a beat, I said, “Playing alone helps me clarify my thoughts.”

“Hmmm.”

Corinne was a master at making cryptic responses guaranteed to get a reaction, but I had no intention of satisfying her curiosity. I rose, and helped her to stand. “Are you driving me to the course or am I leaving you in town?”

“Are you in a hurry?”

“No, why?”

She slid both arms around my neck. “My locs need tightening. I’m going to make a few calls and then head out with you.”

“So about an hour?” I asked, thinking about the three o’ clock meeting I’d scheduled and the fact that I wanted to get in at least nine holes before that.

“Yes, I’ll be ready by then.”

“Good.” I lowered my head to hers and homed in for a kiss. My hands slid down the back of her sundress and cupped her firm bottom. I pulled her closer, which wasn't a good idea because my reaction to her was immediate. With the meeting happening so soon, I couldn't start anything I didn't have the time to finish. I whispered in Corinne's ear. "To be continued later."

"There's no time like the present." She twisted her hips in invitation.

"Agreed, but you have plans to make yourself even more beautiful and I may not get the opportunity to play the White Witch again."

The White Witch was a beautiful, world-renowned golf course situated in Rose Hall.

Corinne patted my chest and stepped away from me. "That's total and utter B.S., but you win. This time."

"I'll make it up to you."

Her hips swayed in a delicious rhythm as she walked across the patio. Over her shoulder, she said, "You'd better, if you know what's good for you."

* * *

The nine holes I hoped to play were shortened to six. The lack of time made that my reality. Despite that, I enjoyed the layout of the course. Bunkers nestled in the undulating land and surrounding lush greens characterized the course that was part of the original estate that belonged to the infamous Annie Palmer, known as the White Witch of Rosehall.

After driving the rest of the holes on the golf cart, I returned to the club house in time to wash my face and order a Red Stripe Light Beer. I tried the sorrel flavor for the heck of it because Corinne liked it. The sugar was slightly too much for me, but I solved that by also purchasing a bottle of water.

When my contact, Dwight Hanes, came into sight, I got to my feet. I'd met him in Miami on another assignment and stayed in touch when I needed his expertise, which was mapping and navigating challenging spaces. Comparing him to a rat wasn't complimentary, but he had a nose for getting in and out of dangerous places. Jamaica was his home base, a blessing in this instance.

We shook hands and sat. He declined my offer of a drink, laid a case on the table, and looked at his watch. "I have a site meeting with a developer after this, so I'm on the clock."

"What can you tell me about the area we want to get into?"

He ran a hand over his goatee while thinking. "For one thing, it's densely populated. For another, it's volatile. It's not uncommon for anything to jump off in a minute. A stranger going in would attract attention immediately. The only possible advantage you'd have is the cover of being lost tourists who like straying off the beaten track."

"But darkness might actually help us," I suggested.

"Agreed, but beware. These people firebomb first and ask questions later." Here, he chuckled. "You don't want to be shot full of holes, so you have to make strategic plans."

Nodding, I said, "That's why we're here."

He stared at me for what felt like a full minute before opening the case, which contained a tablet. "I get that, but you don't know the lay of the land, so..."

"Isn't that what you're about to show me? Plus, I have been here for a few days scoping out the communities."

What I didn't say was that Neil and I had conducted successful rescues with less intel than we had now.

"Yes, but this is only a crash course," Dwight answered. "I'm also saying if you need another pair of hands, let me know as soon you can. I know this area a lot better than you."

"That makes sense." Unwilling to commit this minute since I still needed more information from Neil and Marcus, I added, "I'll let you know. Now, the first thing I want to scope out is all the entry and exit points, plus the main arteries leading to and from the major roads."

Dwight's lips curled in a full smile. "You've always been one for the fine details."

"That's why I've lived this long."

When he chuckled, I did as well. "I'm sure that's why you have, too."

"I won't deny that."

In forty-five minutes, he gave me the "Cliffs Notes" on the community I was planning to slip into, which shared borders with the Caribbean Sea, the Montego Bay business district, another depressed area, and a well-to-do neighborhood. By the time we finished, I had a better idea of what strategy I could employ when the time came to move. Added to that, Dwight provided specialized equipment that would have been hard to bring through customs.

I drove the RAV4 back to the villa since Corinne hadn't yet called. My iPad was in the safe and I didn't care to retrieve it because I had limited time in the bedroom. Instead, I sat in front of Corinne's laptop researching several of the areas Dwight had mentioned. The history, development, and social make-up of the parish of St. James kept me occupied until Corinne rang.

"I'm almost ready," she said, after greeting me. "I wanted to take you to the Doctor's Cave Beach but I forgot to take a bathing suit with me."

"I'm at the villa." I got up and stood at the window overlooking the still water in the pool. "I can bring anything you like."

"Nice. Bring me the black one-piece."

I turned and faced the room, which the staff had set to rights earlier in the day. "Anything else?"

"Towels, and don't forget your bathing trunks."

"I won't."

"How long before you get here?"

"Woman, I haven't left yet, and you know traffic is always bad in Montego Bay."

Corinne chuckled, then said, "Don't take forever."

"I'll do my best, your highness."

She snickered, made a kissing sound, then warned me again not to keep her waiting too long.

I gathered the items she needed, and stuffed them into a beach bag. Then I went to find the housekeeper, Yvonne, who was in the kitchen. “I’m going out again. See you later.”

She gave me a bright smile and stood back from the carrots she was slicing. “Dinner will be ready by six.”

“Thanks, I’ll let Corinne know.”

I made a note to be sure to leave a generous tip. The staff had made our stay extraordinary in the few days we’d been there. They operated in the background and it seemed like whatever we needed that was on the tip of our tongue appeared as if by magic.

They certainly knew their business. I could get used to the idyllic lifestyle we’d been exposed to, with Corinne as my companion. The tranquil existence inside the villa community was a far cry from the details Dwight shared with me an hour ago.

The drive to the city center should have taken me ten minutes, but ended up being twice as long. I didn’t get a chance to park when I reached the shopping center because Corinne stood in front of the main building and waved as I drove up to the sidewalk. She sat next to me and shut the door before I had a chance to move from behind the wheel. “What took you so long?”

I looked sideways at her. “Why are you always in a hurry?”

She laughed. “I asked you first.”

A scan of her face and hair made me pull her closer and peck her lips. The tightened locs had been twisted into a knot on top of her head, and her wine-red lipstick matched the color in her hair. Corinne reminded me of royalty. “You look wonderful.”

“Thank you, kind sir.” An indulgent smile softened her face. I wanted to see that approving light directed at me all the time. “Is that compliment designed to distract me?”

“Of course not. I’ve never told you anything I don’t mean.” As I drove around the lot toward the exit, I glanced at her. “So after all that, you’re going to drench your hair with sea water?”

“Who said anything about getting my hair wet?” Her brows rose as if I’d said something idiotic. “Do I look like I’ve lost my mind?”

"No, ma'am. I guess there's a method to your madness."

"You'd best believe it." She grinned and slid a hand into my lap. "I hope you're wearing those swim trunks."

"You claimed this was the best beach in MoBay, so I wouldn't miss the opportunity."

She squeezed my leg, a mischievous and playful gesture that made me think once again that I could see her in my life on a permanent basis. Corinne was mercurial and passionate, which made life interesting. I wondered if she was aware how much I missed her when we were apart, which was too often for my taste.

We paid the fees and Corinne commandeered a spot on the white-sand beach. The water was an inviting blue-green color which, in combination with the dazzling sunlight, was a recipe for sunburn. Tourists dotted the sand and the water. After Corinne changed into her suit and smeared the two of us with industrial-grade sunblock, we ran to the water. While I swam out to sea, she bobbed close to the shoreline. I headed back, swam out again, then snuck up on her, grabbing her around the waist.

She didn't shriek, but kicked like she intended to do some damage.

"You nearly kicked me in the crotch," I growled in her ear.

Corinne laughed and turned to slip her arms around me. "It's what you deserve for trying to frighten me. Not that you were successful or anything."

"Liar." Gently, I bit the side of her neck. "If you weren't frightened, yet you kicked like a donkey, I imagine they'd be carting me off to the hospital if you were."

We laughed and horsed around in the water, with Corinne cupping and teasing me in a way she shouldn't since there was nothing I could do about it, situated as we were with people around us. I leaned into her, detailing in her ear everything that would happen after we digested our dinner that night.

She shimmied against me and batted her eyelashes. "Seriously? Maybe we should head back to the villa now."

"Talk about being greedy."

"You started it," Corinne said, then sucked my neck.

Although she'd proven slippery in terms of any serious discussion, I tried my luck again. "So, what are we doing about us, Corinne?"

She looked up at me with a tiny frown line marking her forehead. "What d'you mean?"

"Where are we going?"

She hugged me around the shoulders, which meant she didn't have to look at me. Then she spoke into my ear. "I don't have a clue what I'm doing. Do you?"

I bit one edge of my lip to hold in my grin. At least she was being honest and not avoiding the issue. For the moment, I held her close with both hands banded across her back. "Don't worry about it. We'll figure it out together."

She kept her arms wrapped around my body as we bobbed in the water and it occurred to me that maybe, just maybe, Corinne had been avoiding this discussion not because she valued her independence, but because she didn't want to open herself up to being hurt a second time.

As I placed a kiss on her ear, I promised myself I'd do everything to restore her faith. I still hadn't told her that I knew what had happened with Marcus, but the right moment would come to disclose that fact. I hoped she'd think it important enough to tell me at some point.

Corinne's mood was reflective as we drove back to the villa. We showered together and made slow, sweet love without exchanging any words. I helped Corinne, then put her out of the stall to have my own shower.

While I did, I thought about the short time I'd had Rosalie and what life might have looked like if she'd survived until now. Because I couldn't bear that kind of loss again, I'd bounced around all these years. My thoughts threatened to depress me, so I switched them off.

As I walked into the bedroom, I dried the stubble on my head and lowered the towel to my chest. A sinking sensation replaced the weight that had lifted seconds ago.

Corinne was sitting at the laptop. She turned a narrow-eyed gaze on me. "Why are you looking at anything to do with Flankers and Norwood? Since that can't be about a getaway, just what are you planning?"

seventeen

CORINNE SMIRKED ACROSS THE TABLE. "You're attacking that steak as if you haven't eaten in a week."

"The trip to the beach, plus the way you worked me over in the shower left me hungry."

This time a sensuous smile lifted her lips, but she didn't speak.

In the distance, the sounds of the night—crickets, random bird calls, and traffic—-kept us company on the patio.

While I took the last few bites of the succulent beef, Corinne asked our waiter about dessert.

"We have rum and raisin cheesecake this evening," he said.

She beamed at the pot-bellied server dressed in black and white. "That sounds lovely."

I pushed away my plate. "I'll have a slice too."

While we waited, I reached across the pristine white tablecloth and laid my hand on top of Corinne's. Our time in Jamaica would end soon and it was important to let her know I wanted all my tomorrows with her.

As if she read my thoughts, Corinne said, "Our getaway has been great, but I need more."

"What d'you mean?" Although we were alone on the patio, I lowered my voice. "Babe, anything you need, I'm willing to provide."

Her eyes were unreadable as she studied me. "I hope you'll remain in one piece to keep your promises."

"Come on, Corinne, stop putting negative words into the atmosphere." I chuckled. "If I were a superstitious man, you'd have me looking over my shoulder."

She sighed and rubbed the space between her eyes.

"What's wrong? You look worried."

"That's because I am."

While I stroked the back of her hand with my thumb, she said, "You're still frustrating me with your secrets. Fact is, I know you can take care of yourself but you're not invincible. That's cause for concern."

A loud bird call distracted me, and when I looked back at Corinne she was still focused on me. "This is the main reason I've never told you about these assignments. I didn't want you worrying about me when we weren't together."

"I get it, but I wouldn't be so annoyed with you if you'd stop shutting me out."

I opened my mouth to protest and Corinne said, "You do."

The concern in her eyes touched me and after a moment, I said, "As far as I know, right now I'm just doing some advance surveillance. If anything changes, I'll let you know."

One side of her mouth quirked. Then she grinned. "Getting anything out of you is like pulling teeth, but that's a start. And see, I knew you were up to something."

As her eyes twinkled, my heart swelled, and I wanted to pull Corinne into my lap and kiss her until she was breathless. The fact that she cared for me demonstrated what it would be like to have someone to come home to at the end of each day. The longer I looked at her, the more I wanted what I didn't even know I'd been missing. I was about to tell her how much I appreciated her, when the waiter returned with dessert.

As we ate, it was as if I couldn't take my eyes off her. This week cemented the fact that we were good together. She was excellent company, whether we were in conversation or just sharing the same space while doing different activities. She wasn't afraid to say what was on her mind, and her honesty in calling me out kept me grounded. Sex with her was better than good, and looking at her stirred my desire any time of day, no matter what she was wearing.

She slid a forkful of cake into her mouth, then looked at me. Her tongue came out to lick a bit of whipped cream off her lip. The movement stirred memories of our time in the shower, and I shifted to make room in my pants.

Corinne didn't have to do much to make me want her and that, in itself, amazed me. Since we'd gotten together, I hadn't looked at another woman. She had moved past the stage of a casual liaison and I allowed it, unlike the other women who had kept me occupied over the years.

By nature, I wasn't a cheater, but I didn't know when I decided Corinne was the one. It happened when I wasn't looking. That knowledge was what made me ask her to give me more of herself and her time.

Plus, I'd had a near miss in Brazil a month before Zane's christening. I barely escaped with my life, after Neil and I huddled behind a disgusting hovel in a "favela" or ghetto in Rio de Janeiro with bullets whizzing past our heads. The realization that I could die without telling Corinne how special she was to me made it imperative that I talk to her. Six more hours passed before I had the chance to call, and that's when I told her I needed some kind of commitment from her.

You love that woman. You just don't know it, or you haven't admitted it to yourself. If you're not careful, you'll fart around and lose her.

Doug's words slammed me in the chest and I sat motionless, the cream cheese, rum, and raisins forgotten on my tongue.

"Are you okay?" Corinne asked.

I nodded, then after a moment, I said, "Let's take a walk when we're finished."

Under the light of the moon and the flickering candlelight, I helped Corinne out of her chair. With an arm around her shoulders, I guided her to the stone steps and we went down to the beach. The soft wind combined with the waves washing onto the shore was relaxing, and I was content with Corinne's arm around my waist as we strolled through the sand.

While holding the hem of her dress above the water around her calves, Corinne pulled in deep drags of salty sea air and turned her face into the wind, letting the cool air drift over her skin. As I watched her, I was more certain than ever that I wanted her to be part of my forever.

After we returned to the villa, Corinne and I made love in a way we never had before. At first it was hurried and frantic, as if we would soon part company. When our passion cooled a little, our love-making turned slow and deeply sensuous. My hands roamed her body as I kissed her everywhere. She grabbed my arms, keening, and then begging me not to stop what I was doing.

If anyone had told me I would feel this way about another woman in my lifetime, I would have said they didn't know what they were saying. Corinne stirred emotions in me that I thought were long dead, and I admired her attitude and strength.

She had a zest for life that captivated me. I'd seen so much of the ugly side of humanity during extractions that Corinne became a means of escape. I lived for the times when we were together and longed to be with her when we were apart. Now that I'd woken up the reality of how important she was to me, I wanted to be with her all the time.

What we'd do about our living arrangement, I didn't yet know. One thing was certain; if Corinne was prepared to be a permanent part of my life, we'd find a way to make our love work.

eighteen

JUST BEFORE WE were scheduled to leave Jamaica, Neil called and told me to stay put until he arrived. According to the intelligence he received, Jace was definitely here. My scouting hadn't been a waste of time. By this time, we'd been in Jamaica for a week and I figured I'd have to return if we didn't get any more details on Jace and his movements.

Neil had done additional legwork. The telephone numbers we found in Jace's room was not the only copy. Somewhere in Jamaica, a scamming outfit had the same list and were placing calls to vulnerable people in the United States. The targets were mainly people on disability and retired folks. Neil had gotten that much out of Jace before the boy disappeared again. Angella was sure he was in Jamaica and wanted her son out, but didn't want him to be caught in an FBI dragnet.

How the scammers had acquired the Minnesota residents' telephone numbers, we had yet to find out. Knowing Neil, he would have those details by the time he arrived on the island. He was resourceful when it came to getting data that wasn't readily available. His source was an agent inside the FBI.

The challenge that faced me was how Corinne would deal with

me taking part in a full-scale operation when we were supposed to be in vacation mode. We took several tours that included the YS Falls in St. Elizabeth, a natural attraction that featured seven waterfalls. Corinne insisted we also tour the Dunn's River property and climb the falls, which she'd never done although she lived on the island.

I berated myself over getting distracted and neglecting to tell Corinne about my assignment. During the week, I'd kept putting off the fact that it might become a reality. At any moment, I expected a call from Neil, who landed an hour ago. I had shared the details of my meeting with Dwight, so Neil was privy to all the information I received.

Corinne and I were watching an action/adventure movie in an impressive entertainment room fitted with all kinds of doodads. The sound effects were impressive and would probably have frightened people who, according to Corinne, were termed "weak hearts" in Jamaica.

As I watched the heroes firing at militia and blowing up buildings, I acknowledged the events as a romanticized version of what happened during extractions. Half the time nothing went as planned, and we emerged bruised and battered. Sometimes we barely escaped with our lives. I glanced at Corinne and wondered what my life would look like if I gave up these extractions.

After rolling the idea around in my mind for a bit, a satisfied smile curved my lips. If I had Corinne waiting for me after each assignment, I wouldn't run the risks I now did. Perhaps I'd give it up altogether. Over the years, I sometimes thought I had a death wish. With no wife or children to fill my days and nights, sometimes life had looked bleak. But not anymore.

Corinne kissed my jaw and looked up at me. "Why do I feel like you're in la-la land?"

"For your information, I'm very much here."

She laid her head in my lap and went back to watching the movie. I stroked her arm, then ran my fingers through her locs and massaged her scalp. She loved it when I did that, and her soft moan encouraged me to continue.

My mind went back to Jace. The teenager was more resourceful than Marcus and Angella, who had called frantic, a couple of days ago. There wasn't much I could do from Jamaica, which was why I asked Neil to meet with them.

Although the police had rounded up some of the members of Jace's gang, it seemed their operations had continued uninterrupted. If Jace didn't act right, it was only a matter of time before he'd be in police custody, whether here or in Miami.

Lottery scamming was serious business. The criminals called persons on their target list— usually the most vulnerable like senior citizens and those on disability—and informed them they had won the lottery but could only access the funds if they paid a processing fee. The scammers were convincing and, if they didn't get the money they asked for, resorted to harassment and threats. The discovery of how many people were swindled out of their money across the United States staggered me.

Jamaican gangs were of particular interest to the FBI. For all we knew, Carey and his band of criminals were already on a watch list.

Corinne rolled over and looked up at me. "...okay with that?"

"Yeah, sure," I said, although I hadn't heard exactly what she said.

She sat up and faced me. "Really? You're not even paying attention to anything I say to you."

With a rueful smile, I pulled her against my side. "I'm sorry, what did you say?"

"I just had the urge to ask you if everything was all right. I figured you'd zoned out."

"I admit my mind has been drifting."

"I'm not going to ask if it's anything you care to share because you'll slide out of the discussion. The habits of a lifetime are hard to break."

I scratched my cheek and ran a hand over my jaw. "That's true.

But I'm going to be honest and say there are some aspects of the job I'd never dream of discussing with you."

"I get that, and I'm good as long as you don't go back to your Lone Ranger act."

A pang of anxiety attacked my stomach because I needed to tell her that I'd be leaving her for at least a few hours tonight. I kissed the side of her neck and brushed my beard against her cheek. "You mean a lot to me. In fact, you're the first woman who's made me want to try something long term since my wife died."

"If that's the case, it shouldn't be that hard to level with me."

I left the sofa to pace the room while she muted the sound on the television.

Corinne stayed quiet, watching me. When I realized I wouldn't get out of an explanation, I stood before her with my arms folded. My body language would strike her as defensive, so I lowered both hands to my sides.

"Going into the spices and coffee business kept me sane after my wife died." I kept walking, unable to stand the intensity of her gaze. "At first, I wasn't making much money, but within a year, business picked up and I started making a good living. I've always turned a profit since then. My investments have also done quite well, thanks to Doug."

My cell vibrated on the table and I looked down. Neil was calling.

"I have to get that."

Corinne inclined her head toward the phone. "Go ahead."

I barely said my name when Neil cut me off. "The police are going to conduct a raid in the area where Jace is holed up. My information is accurate. We need to get him out."

"How soon is the...?" I caught myself and stopped in time.

"It's an early dawn operation, so we need to get him out now."

"Yeah, I get it." My gaze went to Corinne, whose face was an expressionless mask, as if she knew what was coming.

I ended the call, but didn't make any move to ask the houseman to alert the security team. The estate was gated and had security guards at several points. If the people in the villa didn't expect any visitor who turned up, they wouldn't be allowed inside the property no matter how good their story.

I stood in front of Corinne, who stood and folded her arms. "I'm assuming you have to run off somewhere despite the fact that we were having an important conversation."

"I'm sorry. I forgot—"

"You don't *forget* something like that." She held up both hands to ward off my words. "And to think we were just talking about the way you do things, but don't worry about it. You go do what you have to, but don't expect me to be here when you get back."

Her words poured ice water into my veins and a vise gripped my chest. "I wouldn't go if I didn't have to."

"Frankly, I don't care." She tightened her jaw and stepped sideways. "You don't even know how to be honest."

I circled her arm, but she twisted out of my grip. "Corinne—"

Corinne's eyes flashed fire and her nostrils flared. "Roger, leave me the hell alone."

She stalked out of the room, leaving me to deal with my disappointment. How the hell would I concentrate on the assignment ahead of me when I was worried about what she'd do while I was gone?

Neil was already en route to me. There was no way he could complete the job on his own. I couldn't back out, no matter how much I wanted to appease Corinne. I didn't want it to be this way, but right now, the job threatened to destroy what I'd come to realize I needed most in my life.

nineteen

THE SAME QUALITIES I admired in Corinne also frustrated me. The moment our eyes met, we knew we were interested in each other. I didn't have to cajole or persuade her to go out with me or into taking the next step when that time came.

Corinne knew exactly what she wanted and wasn't afraid to reach for it. That made me admire her more than any other woman. Now that she'd made up her mind about me, my stupidity had put me half a dozen steps backwards from where we'd been this past week.

I leaned against the door jamb of the bedroom we'd shared for the past five nights. She sat with her back against a cluster of pillows. Posed in front of the carved wood headboard with her locs in a topknot and wearing a silky robe, Corinne looked every inch the queen she was. Pity she wasn't giving me the time of day.

When she refused to look up, I sat on the edge of the bed and dropped the bag I carried on the floor. I knew better than to touch her.

She was scrolling on Instagram and still acted as if I was invisible.

The phone on my hip buzzed, but I ignored it. "Corinne, can I ask you to not leave until I return?"

Her gaze flicked from the phone screen to my face. "Give me a reason," she said in a cool voice.

I pulled in a deep breath and dragged a hand over my jaw. "Because I messed up."

She lowered her eyes to the page she was viewing. "Not good enough. You keep doing the same thing and have no intention of changing."

"Cor—"

The phone stopped, then rang again. I didn't answer, but without doing me the courtesy of looking at me, Corinne said, "Duty calls, apparently."

I picked up the small duffel I'd collected from Dwight, which rested at my feet. "We'll talk later. Promise."

Her lips quirked, then she scoffed, as if she didn't expect me to live up to my words.

I stiffened my back and headed for the front door although the bag in my hand felt like it was weighted with my regrets.

The houseman met me in the living room. "Do you know what time you'll be coming back, Mr. Blythe?"

"At this point, I can't say."

He handed me a small gadget with key cards attached. "These are for the gate and the front door."

"Thanks, Barry."

He grinned and saluted me before slipping away as quietly as he'd come.

I went through the front door that they kept wide open until late in the evening because of the security measures they had in place.

Neil waited on the outside and threw me a dirty look when I slid into the passenger seat of the Camry. "It certainly took you long enough. I won't even ask what you were doing all this time."

"That's nunya business, man."

He laughed as we drove off in the direction of the city of Montego

Bay. Throwing me another look, he said, "At least you came dressed for business."

We wore similar clothing—dark, lightweight sweaters and black jeans with workman's boots.

"You have the stuff?" he asked.

I squeezed the bag between my feet. "Yeah, Dwight provided everything we need."

One of the advantages of having partners in the places we visited was that we could afford to travel light. Some items would raise red flags with customs, so we didn't chance bringing them from the States.

Neil focused straight ahead, tapping his horn to let a motorist out of a side road. "The only thing I brought was my Glock."

"No problems through customs?"

"You mean aside from the five thousand questions I had to answer, even after I provided them with a certificate of ownership and my license?"

We chuckled and discussed the strategy we would use to extract Jace and get him on a plane to Miami. As we drew nearer to the community where Jace was located, we went silent. No doubt Neil was doing the same thing as I. Going over our plan of attack.

I didn't need to bring my iPad because the information was burned into my brain, a habit developed from the job. With my phone in hand, I went to Google Maps to be sure we were on track. The amazing thing I discovered was that even in Jamaica, Google Maps was accurate enough to zero in with clear overhead visuals of individual properties.

Neil didn't subscribe to using GPS systems when we were on the ground unless forced. I was under no such restriction.

"Another mile or so will take us to the road where we enter."

I sucked in a deep breath and hauled the bag from between my feet. After pulling out a handkerchief to cover my face, I decided against using it immediately. We didn't know who we'd meet on the way in and I didn't want to be shot up because I looked like a gunman.

Neil turned the car into a road that could have used a coating of asphalt. The vehicle wobbled on the rutted surface, forcing Neil to slow his pace. The streetlights were far apart and bushes lined both sides of the road.

I kept a watchful gaze on our surroundings. It wasn't uncommon to have gang members swarming onto the road. And if we met any of the men connected to the Top Shelf MoBay Syndicate, who ruled the area, we needed to be prepared for immediate action.

We came to an intersection, crept across and were approaching a set of houses when three men stepped out of the bushes and flagged us down. Two of them carried weapons. Given the narrowness of the road and the fact that we were headed deeper into the community, our only option was to stop.

With my feet, I pushed the bag closer to the dashboard and kept both hands positioned on my legs while Neil rolled down the window.

The bearded man, who wore a dark cap pulled down over his eyes, leaned over to speak to Neil. "'Night, where you heading?"

"We're coming from Kingston and were looking for Norwood." Neil's glib lie almost had me smiling.

Until the man responded. "So, don't yuh know is a dangerous t'ing to be driving around at night in a place yuh don' know? Yuh look smarter dan dat." He leaned closer and met my eyes. "What yuh say, boss man? Yuh singin' di same song?"

His companions stood inches away, one at the bonnet, the other at the bumper of the Camry. Each of them had rags pulled over their faces, and caps covering their heads.

The one covering the bonnet peered at us. "Dem don't look like no tourist to me."

Before he got any ideas about telling us to get out of the car, I headed him off. "I have relatives in Norwood and they're expecting us to show up soon. From what I remember, it's about five minutes that way." I pointed, hoping it was the right direction.

He continued staring at us, tapping his gun against his jeans as if longing to do some damage.

I kept my eyes on him, knowing that in every such group, there was one hothead.

The man by Neil's window stood straight. "Stop giving di tourist dem a hard time."

He leaned toward Neil again and cracked a smile. "Go back di way yuh came and go right. The next road will take yuh into di community."

"Thanks, man." Neil grinned big and prepared to reverse.

The guy standing behind the car stepped out of the way. Then the leader of the group put his hand back on the window. I froze, wondering what was up now.

"Turn on yuh headlights. Coming in without any lights in a place like dis can be dangerous to yuh health."

He threw back his head and laughed, while Neil nodded and I gave him a thumbs up sign.

They stood in the road while Neil reversed to the intersection, turned around and headed the other way. None of them made any move and stood as if they owned that stretch of road. I guess they had the run of the place if they could be out at night openly carrying guns. And these weren't just any weapons. These were AK-47s and a Desert Eagle. Expensive fire power that shouldn't have been in the hands of men who didn't seem to be more than community enforcers.

But I knew that these men were led by a "don" who reigned over the community. That man would have more spending power and access to high-quality equipment than the local police could even dream about. Jamaica's geographical position between the U.S. and South America helped gun and drug runners maximize their illegal earnings. Lottery scamming was the new kid on the block in terms of crime, and the biggest money earner.

We made the obligatory left turn before Neil said, "What now?"

Chuckling, I said, "This time, we enter through the front gate."

"Isn't that a little risky to roll up to the entrance of the community? What if we're searched?"

"I have a feeling we'll get past without them searching us, but when we pull up to that bridge, let me cross it."

He threw me a doubtful look as we passed under a street light. "You and your corny clichés."

I couldn't resist throwing in another one. It was my way of easing the tension. "Simply follow my lead if we land in a pickle."

"Whatever, man. Just don't haul off and hit anybody."

I gave him a side-eye. "You're never going to forget that, are you?"

"Nope, not as long as I have to work with you."

Neil was referring to a situation more than a year ago, where the police stopped and detained us in Kingston. One officer had gotten on my nerves and provoked me, then pushed me in the chest, and I landed a blow to his jaw.

That had gotten me thrown in jail overnight. It wasn't an experience I wanted to repeat. The cell had been rank and overcrowded. Lucky for us, we'd been there to collect a rogue embassy employee in a below-the-radar operation and bring him back to the States. The U.S. embassy had smoothed the ruffled feathers with the local police hierarchy, and we left the island having fulfilled our mission.

"When you get to the next intersection, circle back and head the other way."

Neil scoffed as an SUV zoomed past us. "Really?"

"Yes, trust me on this." I pointed over my shoulder. "The main entrance to the community is that way."

"But didn't you say it's under curfew?"

"Well, it was, but I hear it was lifted a few days ago."

Neil glanced at me, then spun the car around under the glare of several street lights. "Is this legit information or are you going on hearsay?"

"Am I a professional, and have I ever led you astray?"

"Hmmm."

I thumped him on the shoulder. "You worry too much. We'll be in and out before you know it."

"I sure hope so." He sat forward in the seat and gripped the wheel tighter. "But this area is volatile and anything can happen before we know it."

"Which is why we're doing this now. Only people up to no good and people like us are out at this hour. Tell me what Jace is doing here. Where did he access that target list?"

"The short answer is from 'lead lists' developed by workers in those customer service call centers." He waited a beat before adding. "Some of these individuals should be held liable for disclosing people's personal details. Lottery scamming is a monster that nets these criminals more than three hundred million U.S. dollars each year."

"That would be why they continue to develop the business."

"True."

As I scanned the roadway, I said, "My research tells me they make thousands of calls each day to swindle people out of their hard-earned money."

"When you're making that amount of money, you give up on ordinary pursuits like school and an education. Jace obviously bought into that get-quick-rich mentality when he linked up with the Miami Top Shelf Syndicate and somehow joined this local arm."

The gangs weren't headed by men with university educations, but were challenging to dismantle. "Sounds like these guys have built and expanded their own corporation."

With his eyes on the road, Neil said, "And each time the local police smashes one crime ring with the help of the FBI, another develops."

We traveled in silence, and soon after Corinne invaded my mind. I wanted this job to be a simple proposition. If we were lucky, we'd be in and out within a forty-five-minute span, maximum. After that,

I'd think about how to win Corinne back, if she was prepared to listen to me.

My focus returned and I pointed to a decorative concrete structure. "Look sharp, man. There's the welcome sign."

We rolled past the painted concrete and continued on the main avenue, another road that didn't deserve that designation. The path was unpaved with potholes stretching as far as our headlights went.

A glance at my watch confirmed it was just after midnight. When I looked back at the rutted track, the street lights were out. I couldn't see anything other than the outline of a tent to one side of the road, along with a metal barrier.

I blew out a deep breath as my skin prickled. "I think we just ran into an unexpected welcome committee."

Neil groaned. "Not again."

As one of the men's boots crunched over the gravelly ground, I spoke out of the corner of my mouth. "Let me do the talking."

twenty

A UNIFORMED MAN motioned us forward and the other came to the driver's window. "Good evening, gentlemen. The area is under curfew. Are you aware of that?"

We greeted them and answered no, while my gaze went to the tent, where a pair of soldiers and several officers in dark uniforms and bullet-proof vests seemed to be packing up their equipment. Either they were winding down their activities for the night, or were in the middle of a shift change.

My attention swiveled back to the policeman on my side of the car when he shone the light in my face. "D'you have anything to declare?"

I wanted to declare that he had no manners to be shining that high beam in my eyes, but didn't. In my line of work, I understood that while the majority of law enforcement officers dealt with law-abiding citizens, a small percentage did not. Apparently, I looked like I fell in the latter category.

I played it cool and responded to his question. "No, sir."

"Where are you headed at this late hour?"

Somewhere close by, the sound waves from a boom box pounded

the air—the perfect excuse, right when we needed it. "My cousin lives in the area."

The policeman glanced at the other officer, then back at me. "That's convenient. Why are you visiting at this hour of night?"

With my head cocked toward the music, I said, "You hear dat? Dat's why."

I laced my voice with my version of a Jamaican accent. I'd listened to and imitated Corinne often enough—to her combined amusement and annoyance—to sound like I might have left the island as a child. Or so I thought.

Apparently, my accent was entertaining. They chuckled, but the officer armed with the rifle didn't relax and kept his weapon trained on the ground.

"Is that right?" the officer asked.

I smiled wide and bobbed my head. "Yep, it's all about di dance-hall tonight."

"The party won't last much longer. Remember, this is a zone of special operation."

His explanation concurred with what Corinne told me. Jamaica was a place where most obeyed the law and some flouted it at their peril. Under curfew conditions, people were not allowed to gather in public places beyond a certain time of night. Yet, I was sure the party in progress wouldn't end any time soon.

The officer standing by Neil's window gave us another once over and when his eyes met mine, I saw the suspicion in his. "Can I see some identification?"

My response was smooth and fast. "I left my wallet at home."

He stared at me as if he didn't believe a word.

Neil put both hands on the wheel, then pointed toward the dash-board. "Can you reach my stuff?"

The policeman on my side tipped his rifle higher.

Since I had no desire to end the night with a hole shot through me, I took my time about opening the compartment and pulling out the pouch inside. Once I handed it over, Neil took out his wallet and gave it to the man outside the window.

He studied Neil's driver's license and a business card in minute detail before handing them back. "Enjoy your night."

"Thanks, officer."

Neil gave me back the pouch and I stashed it where I found it.

The men stepped away and we drove off, staying silent until we were halfway down the road.

"Why d'you have your personal identification with us in this car?" I chided.

"You're forgetting I just got off a plane. Didn't have time to do more than leave my luggage in the room I rented."

My response was terse. "You know the drill. Don't get careless."

As a practice, when we were in certain situations, neither of us took proper identification just in case we were caught at the wrong place in an unfortunate incident. A few years ago, a lost driver's license could be used as a means of ID by the wrong person to get on a plane to the States, and in some cases could lead criminals to our homes. Everything we carried was fake.

I pointed Neil toward the next corner. He turned into a rutted roadway similar to the one we'd been on a while back. We were halfway down the street when we came to a group of men playing dominoes and carousing in front of a bar. As we rolled past, they went motionless, as if they thought we were up to no good. Although it wasn't a common occurrence, drive-by shootings had been on the uptick in Jamaica in recent times.

I kept an eye on the group as we continued on our way. After a left turn, we came upon another gathering. Massive speaker boxes faced the road and a crowd spilled out of a bar onto the sidewalk.

Some partygoers danced in the middle of the street. Fragrant smoke poured skyward from metal drums on the curb. The aroma of jerked chicken and pork made my mouth water despite the fact that I'd eaten earlier. Huge soup pots stood on make shift stoves constructed from tire rims welded to metal legs.

The coals glowed a bright orange, fueling the steam coming from the pots. I imagined they contained gut-turning items like scraped goat heads, entrails, and other body parts. The locals called the soup mannish water. Corinne told me goat head soup was well-loved, but I'd never understood how she stomached the stuff. Even Doug had developed a taste for it. The other thing Corinne introduced me to was cow cod soup, that was made from a bull's genitals. My face twisted at the thought of what that eating experience might be like.

It took us a while to maneuver through the crowd of mostly young people, some of whom were scantily dressed. Others wore brand name shoes, caps, and clothing. Women gyrated to dancehall music with little regard for our Camry cruising by. Experience told me this street party would continue until daylight, or until the police shut it down in keeping with the nighttime noise ordinances. That's if the customers didn't become unruly and start a riot.

When we made it past the crowd and drove halfway down the block, I asked Neil to park the car in the next slip road. He chose a spot on the soft shoulder under a patch of trees. The black car was almost invisible, which suited us. I unsnapped the seatbelt and reached for the bag. "We go on foot from here."

Neil looked at the incline next to the car, then back at me, wearing a slight smile. "You don't say."

I opened the bag and got out the equipment inside while Neil opened the trunk and stepped into the cool air. Then I strapped on the items we would need, including wire cutters, a large hanky, zip ties, and several canisters.

When we were armed and suited up with gas masks, Neil and I nodded at each other. We must have looked like two aliens about to do some damage to unsuspecting victims. After we touched fists, I beckoned to him and he followed me up the gentle slope toward the house where Jace had been living since he arrived in Jamaica.

The image of the interior layout Dwight provided was etched on my brain. Though we moved in the moonlight, I was confident of the lay of the land. Approaching from the back would give us an element of surprise. Aside from a pack of young, unemployed men involved in a criminal enterprise, I wasn't aware of any security or potential danger on the property where we were headed.

We trotted in a diagonal line. In five minutes, we stood at the end of the small property. The house was a one-story concrete structure that hadn't seen a coat of paint in a while. I eased up to a window and came away with white residue on my sleeve. No lights were on inside, but the moon shed rays across the kitchen floor. A tiny but powerful flashlight helped me scope out the small room.

Neil touched my shoulder and indicated we would do a short reconnaissance and meet at our starting point when we finished. I crept around to the left side and Neil took the right. The trees shading the house provided enough cover for me not to feel exposed.

A barking dog made me stand still. The noise came from across the road and devolved into a series of howls. Corinne had told me when that happened, the hound was seeing something from the spirit world. The thought sent a chill up my spine, but I shook it off. That woman had a way of infiltrating my thoughts at the most inopportune times.

There were two windows on my side of the house, and I gathered all the information I could in one visual sweep. A couple of cots stood against the walls in one room and a sleeping figure occupied each bed. I believed a third bed stood under the window. The front room contained a double bed, and a sheet covered whoever was on the bed. From the size and contour under the fabric, I figured a couple slept there. An empty crib occupied the far corner.

Grille work covered the verandah, which satisfied me. The people inside would have nowhere to run when we cornered them. I returned to the back door where Neil waited for me. In our own sign language built on necessity, he let me know there were a total of six males in two bedrooms. That amount of men in one place couldn't mean anything good. From what I knew, they weren't family and had simply formed an alliance to carry out their nefarious deeds.

Neil and I carried what we needed in hand and stormed the door that was little more than plywood. One well-placed kick and it fell flat on the tiles. From his position in the doorway, Neil lobbed a canister of tear gas inside.

Ten seconds later, the house erupted in movement. Among the expletives came the sound of running feet and agonized moans. We went through the house, shoving people out of the way who stumbled around trying to get their bearings in the smoke-filled rooms. In my earlier years I had been exposed to tear gas, and it was an unpleasant experience, consisting of burning eyes, lungs, and disorientation.

A man emerged from the bedroom on my right, crouched low to the ground, covering his mouth and nose. We ran smack into each other and when he recovered, he shoved me in the chest.

Without hesitation, I gave him a fist to the face. He crumpled to the ground. By the sound of pandemonium around us, everyone was now awake, and it didn't take long to find Jace. He sat on the edge of a cot, then rose to his feet with both arms stretched in front of him. The mask allowed me to pinpoint his slender frame. The mop of curly hair on top of his head and the fade on the sides readily identified him. He stood upright, then squealed like a pig being butchered while rubbing his eyes and nose.

A bag lay on the floor next to the bed he'd been sitting on, and I picked it up.

Through his hacking cough, he cried, "Hey!"

I grabbed him by the shirt and shoved the bag to his chest. He grabbed it and continued coughing and moaning. As we moved toward the door, I hung on to him.

Jace struggled to get out of my hold, but I had him in a firm grip by the back of his zipped hoodie and didn't intend to let him go.

Neil marched in our direction as a man ran out of a bedroom behind him.

The flash of fire lit the passage before I heard the gunshot.

twenty-one

THE BULLET MISSED NEIL, who immediately spun around and kicked the gun from the assailant's hand. My arm burned, which told me I'd been hit, but I had a job to do and was going to complete it. I sprinted from the house, dragging Jace with me. We ran downhill with him fighting me every inch of the way.

The crack of gunshots split the night air and worried me, but Neil could take care of himself. A glance over my shoulder proved that point. He stopped and fired at the men chasing us. At close range, he never missed. This time, he did. But I knew he intended to shoot shy of his target. We weren't here to create any casualties. Our mission was to get who we came for and move out, leaving as little destruction as possible.

The men fled in the opposite direction, and Neil fired a series of shots for good measure.

I hurried toward the car, reassured by the pounding of his feet in the loose stones behind us. Now I was even more grateful for the noise coming from the sound boxes down the road. The gunshots would have carried a longer distance without the heavy music.

Another few minutes brought us back to where we left the car. Neil unlocked the Camry, and I shoved Jace into the backseat and got in beside him. We removed our gas masks and Neil threw them into the trunk. He slid into the car and peeled away from the pulsing deejay music, jostling us in the seat. We headed away from the point where we entered the community, which took us toward the city and the airport.

If he could have killed me with a look, Jace would have done exactly that. I couldn't hide a grin when I said to him, “You don't look surprised to see me.”

He sucked his teeth. “They just don't get it, do they? I don't want to be where they are.”

I could have uttered a thousand words but kept my mouth shut. In this line of work, I’d handled dozens of ungrateful young people with no clue about the sacrifices their parents made to keep them fed, healthy, and educated. This scene was no different.

Peering into the darkness, Neil said, “Your parents want you back, and that's that.”

“He's not my father,” Jace spat.

“Despite that, you're going home.” Neil’s firm response didn’t invite any argument.

Jace uttered a string of local curse words so vile, I winced.

“What the hell did he just say?” Neil asked.

My disgust carried in my voice when I answered, “Trust me, what he said can’t be translated.”

“If you know what's good for you,” I said to Jace, “you’ll keep a low profile.”

“That's right,” Neil added while fiddling with the front of his vest. “You don't want to have to explain to the local police what you were doing with these.” He raised one hand, in which he held several small books.

Sitting forward, I asked, “Are those what I think they are?”

I reached for the three Jamaican passports and turned them over in my hands, which were still covered by a pair of gloves. “They may be fraudulent.”

“Ya think?” Neil’s tone was dry.

"Those have nothing to do with me," Jace groused, while sniffling and clearing his throat.

Neil and I knew the passports likely contained fraudulent visas for the gang members to gain access to U.S. ports with ease.

"Maybe we should stop at the next police station and let them ask you why you were in that house and why you happened to be in the same place as these babies." This time, Neil held up a cheap phone, or a banger, as Jamaicans called them. Then, he held a wad of papers in the air.

Among Neil's specialized skills was the ability to home in on critical items in places like the house we left minutes ago. I assumed the papers were call lists. The phone logs would provide evidence of the activities the men in the house had been engaged in, as soon as Neil scrolled through them.

"Let me tell you something," Neil continued, moving his thumb between himself and me. "People like us have connections everywhere, including the local police department. Don't push your luck."

Jace slumped next to me and folded both arms over his chest. "They still don't belong to me."

"Have you ever seen the inside of a Jamaican prison?" I asked.

Jace didn't answer, but I continued speaking. "You do not want to be locked up in a place where you can get killed for stepping on someone's foot. This may be a game to you, but let me assure you, what you're involved in isn't child's play."

Jace sat unmoving, but his attitude hadn't gone anywhere. The rebellion was churning inside him, but that was okay. As long as we delivered him in one piece, that's all I cared about.

I pointed to his bag. "Get out your passport."

My arm and shoulder throbbed and blood seeped into my sweater. I pulled out a hanky, gritted my teeth, and pressed the square of fabric to the wound.

Jace grumbled, but with the agony searing my arm, I was in no mood to take any foolishness from him. "You heard me. Take it out."

While fussing under his breath, he did what I told him.

I handed Neil the passport over the seat.

"Here's how this is going to play out." I held Jace's gaze in the intermittent light. "My friend here is going to get you on a flight back to Miami. You are *not* going to act like a petulant child during this process. Do you hear me?"

His nostrils flared, but he nodded.

"If you doubt I'm serious, I *will* ensure customs puts you on a watchlist. The next time you try to enter the island, they'll be on the lookout for you for drug running and lottery scamming. Those are the lists your name will be on. I'll make sure of it. You do not want that kind of heat. If you run again, we'll find you. Same as we found you tonight."

He turned wide eyes on me, questioning whether I had the clout to do what I threatened.

A sinister smile eased across my lips and I nodded. "Yes, that's what's in your future if you don't get straight and act right."

Jace shuffled across the seat and stared through the other window. Although he was getting on my last nerve, I felt compelled to try and make him see sense. Perhaps my soft spot had to do with the fact that my niece Mo had been acting up for years, but the little girl she'd been was still somewhere inside her. I got glimpses of it when she let her guard down, and I sensed the young man beside me was trying to find himself but going about self-discovery the wrong way. His parents needed to help him sort himself out before he self-destructed.

"Jace." He turned his head, and I looked him in the eyes. "I know you don't want to hear this, but life is about much more than preying on unsuspecting people and getting a leg up on old folks. You're better than that."

He ignored me, then in a tone dripping with resentment he asked, "Why d'you do this? Isn't it for the money?"

"Partly."

His expression didn't change but after a few more seconds, he said, "What other reason d'you have for chasing people and forcing them to go where they don't want to be?"

I let him wait for my answer, wincing as I kept steady pressure on the gunshot. "Satisfaction. Seeing people reunited. Bringing families together."

"Right. That's bullshit," Jace spat. "You're in it for the cash. What are they paying you for this?"

"Way less than the trouble you're worth," Neil said over his shoulder. "And if you don't cultivate some respect, I'll stop this car in a minute and throw you on the side of the road."

Jace sucked his teeth. "Nah, man, you're not about to lose your meal ticket."

"You're bitter for someone so young." Neil was quiet for a moment, then added, "It doesn't look good on you."

Grumbling under his breath, Jace sank even lower in the seat.

A car swerved toward the Camry from the oncoming lane. Neil jammed the brakes and flung us forward. "Sorry."

I grabbed the back of the seat and a groan escaped from me.

Neil flashed me a glance. "You okay, man?"

"I got hit back there."

He swiveled his head toward me, then looked at the road. "And you didn't say anything?"

"I'll be fine." The handkerchief was wet and blood soaked the sweater on my right side.

"Is it a flesh wound?" Neil asked.

"No, I think the bullet may be lodged in my shoulder."

He swerved onto the soft shoulder, leaned sideways, and got his phone out of the dashboard, then handed mine to me. "I'm going to call a friend."

"Isn't that risky?"

He put the phone to his ear. "I have many talents, but pulling bullets out of people isn't one of them."

When I attempted to speak, he put up one finger and exited the Camry. The odd car passed every so often and several minutes later,

Neil climbed back into the vehicle. “We’re going to get you fixed up. Then Jace and I will head back to Miami.”

I needed a minute with Neil to find out where we were headed and who we’d be seeing. If I turned up at the hospital with a bullet inside me, they were obligated to report it to the police, but I didn’t fancy being operated on by a quack. Since we were now in Rose Hall, I guessed it wouldn’t be long before I’d be patched up. I itched to call Corinne but couldn’t until this job was finished. The minute I got out of the car, that’s what I’d do.

We turned into Ironshore, the same area where Corinne and I were staying. Much of the night had gone and I wondered if I was on her mind in the same way that she wouldn’t leave my thoughts. Only discipline prevented me from calling her now. That, and the fact that she might be asleep. She wouldn’t take kindly to me waking her up just to say hello. Not after the way I left.

“Gimme a minute.” Neil climbed out and ran into the multi-story apartment complex we pulled into that stood next to a hotel.

While we waited, my mind circled to Corinne, and as the blood oozed from my shoulder, I longed to hear her voice and wanted the certainty of knowing she’d be waiting for me, no matter where I went.

Neil approached the car, carrying a brown duffle. He opened the front passenger door and dropped the bag on the floor. “You hanging in there?” he asked when he stood straight.

“Yeah, but you better move fast before I lose every drop of blood.”

“We’ll be there in two minutes.”

We drove to a gated complex of townhouses. After Neil explained to the security guard who we were there to see, we drove in and parked. Then Neil gathered our gear, picked up my bag, and approached one of the houses. The door opened and someone took the bag. Neil returned, helped me out of the car, and locked the door behind me, leaving Jace inside.

“Thank God you didn’t bleed all over the seat. Only the Lord knows what the rental company would think if I brought it back smeared with blood." He studied my sweater, then looked me in the eyes as we approached the building. "You gonna be all right, man?"

"I'll be fine."

Neil angled his body so the car was in view while he introduced me to the tall man with dark-chocolate skin, who stood in the doorway. "Eric, meet Roger. Roger, this is Eric." With one finger, Neil pointed to each of us. "He's good people and you're in excellent hands."

If Neil gave Eric high marks, it meant I could trust him. I patted my partner's shoulder. "Thanks, man."

"Call Corinne now," he said before walking down the path to the car. When he got there, Neil escorted Jace to the front seat before they drove off.

Eric led me to the back of the spacious townhouse, where a study opened into a private surgery. An examination table occupied the middle of the tiles. A desk, two chairs, and a standing lamp were the only other pieces of furniture in the small room. Cream blinds covered the windows. "Sit over there. I'll be with you in a minute."

While holding the soaked material to the wound, I took my phone out and speed dialed Corinne's number, overwhelmed by the need to hear her lyrical accent and throaty tone. When she didn't answer, my breath seeped out and I lowered my head. I rang twice more. Still, she didn't pick up the call.

Eric came back into the room and picked up a pair of scissors. "Let's get you out of this sweater and see the extent of the damage."

"Sure." I laid the phone on the table next to me, hoping Corinne would call me back. With everything in me I prayed she hadn't left the villa, but an echo of doubt reverberated in my mind.

She warned you that she'd go, and you didn't give her a good reason to stay.

twenty-two

SUNSHINE PEEPING through the curtains slanted across the bed and invaded my eyelids. My shoulder throbbed as if someone had broken off a poison dart inside it. I hadn't even opened my eyes properly and the pain went up by several notches. Eric had warned me the wound would be sore when I woke. The room around me was done up in several shades of cream and gold. The king-size bed I lay on and the large sofa in the corner, plus the massive dresser, told me this place had been decked out by a professional decorator.

I reached for the phone on the bed beside me to see if I had missed any calls. A mixture of relief and anxiety curdled in my chest. Neil hadn't called, which meant he and Jace had gotten off the island without any complications. I'd contact him later to see how their flight had gone. I also needed to speak to Marcus. Since Jace was determined to do his own thing, they would have to find an effective way of keeping him in line. His mother wasn't up to that task.

Groaning a little, I sat up. My shoulder muscles complained, but I ignored the shafts of pain as I speed dialed Corinne's number.

This is Corinne. Please leave a message and I'll get back to you when I can.

My stomach was leaden, but I told myself that maybe she hadn't heard the cell. It was after ten o'clock, so maybe she went for a swim or a walk on the beach, although she preferred to do those activities early in the morning.

My next option was to call the villa directly. A quick search in my phone ended with me doing exactly that. The houseman answered and I told him what I wanted.

"I'm sorry," he said. "Miss Corinne is not here."

"Is she down on the beach?"

"No, she left about an hour ago." After a slight pause, he added, "She took her suitcase."

A stabbing pain took root behind my eyes and I rubbed my forehead with one hand. The news that she left gutted me. It wasn't that I hadn't taken her threat seriously. I simply hoped she would have allowed us room to talk like I promised before I left last night.

He made a sound in his throat and my mind returned to the present. "Thank you. I'll see you in a while."

"Will you be having lunch here, sir?" he asked.

"No."

I owed Corinne an apology for my clumsy handling of my departure last night. Still massaging my forehead, I debated what to do. First, I dialed her home number. It was a long shot, but if she was headed to Kingston, she would know that I had called when she got there. Then it occurred to me that she wouldn't go home. We were scheduled to leave Jamaica the following day on a flight from Montego Bay.

Eyes closed, I lay across the bed feeling as if I'd lost myself. I had assumed too much.

I sprang off the mattress and went to the bathroom. After splashing water on my face, I brushed my teeth with a new toothbrush I found on the countertop. I walked back into the bedroom, and that's when I noticed a T-shirt hanging on the closet door handle. Eric had probably left it there last night when he showed me the room. I slipped it over my head and put on my pants.

Phone in hand, I ventured downstairs. I didn't find a soul in the living area, which had a yellow-gold theme like the bedroom. Calling Eric's name, I went toward the back of the house and tapped on the door to the mini-surgery where he treated me last night.

"Coming."

In a couple of seconds, Eric opened the door. This morning he wore a golf shirt, a pair of jeans, and loafers on his feet.

"How are we this morning?" he asked.

"Aside from feeling like someone shattered my shoulder with a sledgehammer, I'll be okay."

"At least your sense of humor is intact." Eric chuckled and pointed at the table. "Sit there and let me look at the wound."

I did as he asked and tried not to wince while he examined my shoulder.

When Eric finished, he re-bandaged the area. "You should be good as new in a few weeks. In the meantime, avoid aggravating your shoulder. I'm going to write a prescription for pain medication. Please take them until they're finished. You should also get your doctor to look at the wound once you're back in the States, to make sure it's healing properly."

I thanked him while we walked back to the living room, then stood by the front window, contemplating the well-manicured grass just beyond the building. "By the way, you haven't told me what all of this costs."

His eyes crinkled when he smiled. "You don't need to pay me anything. I owe Neil a favor or two, so this is one less thing on my tab."

"Understood." I held out my hand and he shook it. He passed me a tiny envelope. "These will take care of the pain until you fill the prescription."

"Thanks again."

"D'you want something to eat before you leave?" he asked.

My stomach growled, but I said, "I don't want to put you to any trouble."

"It's not a problem. My housekeeper has been here for several hours and already cooked breakfast."

"In that case, I'll eat before I go."

We exchanged a grin and he led me to a large kitchen, furnished with what looked like every modern convenience known to man. Impressive, for someone I assumed was a bachelor.

A stout, clear-skinned woman stood at the sink.

"Clara, meet Roger. He'll be having breakfast," Eric said.

"Have a seat, please." Wearing a friendly smile, she asked, "Coffee or tea?"

"I'll have coffee, thanks."

"See you in a bit," Eric said, on his way out of the room. "When you're ready, I'll call a cab."

I inhaled the rich, dark brew Clara set before me and declined the sugar and creamer she offered.

Another thing that reminded me of Corinne. She took her creamer with sugar and coffee, as she jokingly told me several times. I was the exact opposite. I couldn't stand to have my coffee diluted with condiments. According to her, drinking black coffee was like swallowing drain cleaner. The thought brought a smile to my lips. I pictured her clearly in my head, wrinkling her face in disgust. The urgency to find her and resolve our issues gnawed at my gut. I wanted breakfast to be over so I could go find my woman.

The only reason I was sitting around was because I hadn't eaten since dinner early yesterday evening and after last night's events, I was famished. If I passed out from hunger, I wouldn't be of use to myself or anyone else.

The breakfast of callaloo and codfish with green bananas and fried dumplings filled me up. I forced myself to eat all of it because I wasn't sure when I'd have lunch.

The meal was delicious and soon after that, I thanked my host again and was on my way in the back of an air-conditioned cab. The ride to the villa took less than ten minutes, and when I stood in the room Corinne and I had shared for the past week, I felt lost.

Nothing remained to remind me of her, except for the note she left on the desk in her neat cursive.

Not sure where I am headed. I'm sure you will be fine without me.

Her words stung. The days we spent together changed the way I saw my future. I wouldn't be content unless she was part of my life. Corinne had filled the barren spaces and emptiness I'd been ignoring for years. And, after turning my heart upside down, she'd abandoned me. *Us*, really.

Suddenly, I was angry but didn't know who I was more upset with—Corinne, for giving up, or myself for letting her walk away. We were tighter than we'd ever been. Until my job got in the way, once again.

I opened the glass door to the patio and stared at the sky, painted in blues and greens. My thoughts turned to the conversations we had about her favorite places. I narrowed my options to three locations she'd mentioned. Gambling had never been part of my life, but I was willing to bet Corinne had gone to one of two places, if she hadn't left the island.

I was fairly sure she hadn't done that. We were due to return to Miami tomorrow on the same flight, and she didn't believe in wasting money. She wouldn't undo her flight plans. Still, I couldn't be sure because she was like a chameleon. If she didn't want to see me, nothing would stop her from adjusting her itinerary.

With a sense of urgency, I entered the room and picked up my phone.

Corinne could run but she couldn't disappear, not when my specialty was locating people who didn't want to be found. Now that I'd found the one person I didn't want to live without, I wasn't about to lose her.

I speed dialed Doug's number instead of calling Khalila directly. He'd be more likely to answer, but it was critical that I talk to his other half. If anybody knew where Corinne had gone, it would be Khalila. She, more than anyone else, wanted this thing between Corinne and me to work. As such, she'd help me convince my woman that I was worth another chance.

twenty-three

MY DECISION TO leave was rooted in self-preservation. Roger might think I was downright selfish. But it didn't matter. I was taking care of myself. And yet if I was honest, I would admit to running scared. Scared of putting my emotions on the line. Scared of sharing more of myself with Roger. Point blank scared of anything happening to him. If he died, I'd be alone. The same way I'd be if he walked away from me.

If I explained my fears I might sound stupid, but to me they made perfect sense. For a long time I convinced myself I didn't need anyone, and to a certain extent, this was true. I earned my own money, owned my home, and came and went as I pleased.

Roger had changed all that. He eroded my defenses without me realizing how much my outlook had changed in a few months.

Corinne, who never let the grass grow under her feet, was now mired in something she wasn't sure was meant for her.

Call it cowardice, but I switched off my phone the moment I left the villa. Last night, I hoped Roger would take me seriously and abort whatever mission he came to Jamaica to complete. Having told him what I would do if he didn't stay, I couldn't back away from my ultimatum. In the light of day I might have been unreasonable, but

I'd gone too far down this road to turn back. To get away fast, I took the RAV4 Roger had rented and assumed Neil would have Roger covered for a ride.

I hadn't figured out the logistics of flying back to Miami as yet since we had planned to travel together. Only the thought of wasting the money kept me from canceling my booking. At the same time, I had no idea what I'd say to Roger when he caught up with me.

On impulse, I turned my phone back on. As expected, he'd called me a half-dozen times. I felt confident he wouldn't be able to get hold of me because I hadn't left him any clues as to where I was going. The weak link in this equation was Khalila. Deliberately, I hadn't told her where I was headed when I spoke with her this morning to let her know I'd be on the road.

"Where is Roger and why do I feel you're about to do something crazy?" she asked.

"He left last night and I haven't seen him since." My delivery was cool, as if I wasn't seething.

"You definitely plan to do something crazy," Khalila said, her tone resigned. "I don't know what happened between the two of you, but isn't it better to talk through your disagreements? That's what you've always advised me to do, right?"

"In this situation, rehashing things won't work." I let a sigh drop between us and explained last night's disaster. "Trust me, you would also have a problem with the way Roger acts."

"Isn't it better to wait until he comes back and then have it out with him?"

"Lila, I've made up my mind. I just wanted you to know that I'm okay, in case he calls."

Seconds went by before she spoke. "Aside from being annoyed with him, I think you're scared, but you don't need to be. The two of you want each other. You both need to admit it."

I didn't bother to tell her that Roger had come clean about his missing-in-action stints and how I'd been hopeful we would settle into something resembling a normal relationship. So much for that.

Instead, I warned her to stay out of my business and advised her that Doug should do the same.

With a snide chuckle, she said, “I'm not sure how I can be in your business if you're not telling me where you're going.”

“Don’t worry about it. If you're in the dark, then there's no possibility of you blabbing to Roger about my whereabouts. Love you, Lila.”

“Love you, too, Corinne.” She sounded as if I was about to disappear from the face of the earth. “You know I wouldn't let you down.”

“That's all well and good for you to say now, sweetie. Consider this as me protecting you. If I say where I'm going and you tell that man, I might have to kill you.”

She laughed and we ended the call with me promising to be in touch shortly.

In my HR job, I'd come to know many people. I was headed to a small guest house that belonged to one of our clients. I made the call this morning and had gotten a room without having to go through the hassle of making a reservation. I planned to enjoy the Seven Mile Beach, which was reputed to be as long as its name and characterized by soft, white sand, calm blue waters, and a panoramic view of the Caribbean Sea. I’d also watch the sunset, and get a spa treatment while deciding what to do tomorrow.

Khalila would tell me I wanted to control every minute of my day, but it was my view that if I seized it with determination, I could wrangle it in the direction I wanted it to go.

The phone rang, startling me. Roger was at the other end. The unique ringtone I assigned to him clued me in. I let it go to voicemail. Talking to him wouldn’t be a wise move. Roger could be persuasive.

I was vulnerable because aside from my fear of commitment, I was also petrified of being hurt again.

Five minutes later, the phone rang. I looked away from the road to the cell.

Roger was calling again.

I refused to answer.

Minutes later, the same thing. Again, I chose not to speak to him.

Then, he sent a text.

Against my better judgment, I pulled off the side of the road to see what he wanted.

He'd typed two sentences. *I love you. Answer the phone.*

My eyes blurred, and it was a good thing I'd stopped on the soft shoulder. Otherwise, I'd have endangered myself and perhaps other motorists. I pressed the back of my fingers to my eyes.

Roger had done me dirty by weaseling past my defenses with those three simple words. Except for Khalila and my mother, no one had said that to me in more years than I could count. How did he know exactly what would get to the deepest part of me? How was I supposed to run from him when he just hamstrung me?

When he called again, I bit my lip and looked at the phone. Finally, I worked up the courage to answer.

"Yes, Roger." To my own ears I sounded tired.

"Corinne, I'm headed to Negril, and you'd better be at that guest house when I get there."

My mouth fell open. "How—?"

"Never mind how I know where you're going." The blast of a car horn made me miss some of his words. "...Don't make me chase you all over this island. Please. We have to talk."

My lips seemed to have been glued together, so I listened while Roger continued.

"I don't know how to convince you that I need you." When I didn't answer, he sighed. "One thing I do know is that I have to see you face to face to accomplish that."

"Roger, I—"

"I have to get off the phone. I'll see you in a while, okay?"

I couldn't muster much energy, other than to say, "Sure."

"You could sound a little less like you're going to the gallows." Roger released a low chuckle. "But I'll take what I can get."

"Roger, wait—" My words came too late. Roger was gone.

The sparkling turquoise waves just beyond the shoreline seemed to wink at me, reflecting the starburst of hope inside me. Who was I kidding? I was confident, independent and smart. Needing or loving Roger didn't mean I was losing part of myself, which I also dreaded.

A smile pulled at my mouth. Admitting how I felt about him signaled that I'd been slowly healing. Considering where I'd been for the last ten years, that was progress. I sniffled, then gripped the steering wheel and put the RAV4 in motion.

Only God knew what Roger had planned, but I couldn't wait to see him. I inhaled, conjuring the unique and manly scent I'd come to associate with him. I could almost feel the stubble on his jaw against my cheek and his strong arms wrapped around me. He made me feel safe and protected. No other man ever had that effect on me.

Roger had truly done a number on me, and I couldn't see my future without him in it.

twenty-four

ROGER'S AURA reached out to me before I caught him watching me from the patio of the guest house. I sat on a bench on the beach, but even from that distance, I felt the intensity of his gaze. I stared at him just as hard.

My attention drifted to the white T-shirt he now wore. What happened to the sweater he was wearing when he left yesterday? His pants were also different. Yet, I was fairly certain he hadn't taken any clothing with him. He needed to shave, but otherwise, he seemed fine.

When he pulled his hands out of his pants pockets, he winced but his gaze didn't leave me while he crossed the polished planks. The urge came over me to leave my seat, race across the sand, and wrap my arms around him. I was surprised to discover that I had actually missed him.

The way he scoured me with his eyes told me he felt the same way.

A soft smile tipped my lips up without my permission. Although still upset with him, I was past the stage where I needed to play childish games. Nothing would be achieved by it.

He sat next to me on the worn wooden bench and stared out to sea. The tree above us dappled our skin as the leaves shifted in the breeze.

After a moment, Roger folded my hand inside his. “Have you decided which mountain I have to climb and which sea I have to swim before I can get back in your good graces?” His low, melodious voice washed over me in a welcome wave, until his words made sense to my brain.

I looked at him sideways. “You have a nerve, considering.”

“You need nerves of steel to do what I do.” He shrugged. “It comes with the territory.” When I tried to interrupt, he added, “Plus, if I wasn’t an exceptionally strong man, there's no way I could be with you.”

“I hope you realize you're not helping your case.”

He looked me in the eyes. “If I didn't believe in what I'm about to do or that I had even a slim chance at success, I wouldn't be here.”

“Be that as it may...”

Roger shot me a quelling look.

The wind came up, and I gathered the material of my dress between my thighs for decency’s sake.

“What’s the matter?”

“You come up with that B.S. phrase whenever you want to hide from me.”

I didn’t answer but simply basked in the silence for a few more minutes. The breeze caressed my face and threaded through my hair. I dug my toes into the warm sand, expectant and yet apprehensive about getting to the crux of the matter between us.

“How did you find me?”

“Remember that conversation we had last year, when you told me of two places where you felt most peaceful? And the one place where you’d like to own some property?”

I sighed, then nodded. This man had the power to pull information out of me that I hesitated to share with anyone but Khalila. He’d done it again that time.

“One was Portland, because you love the atmosphere, and the

other was this place in Negril. I figured you wouldn't stray too far because of our travel plans." The wind swept around us and the shouts of the tourists carried to us. "But knowing you, I prepared myself just in case I had to find my way to the other end of the island, minus my means of transport."

"So, how did you get here so fast?"

"I rented a car from another company."

"Sorry about that. I'll make it up to you." After a deep breath, I asked, "Where did you go last night?"

Roger got to his feet and took my hand. "Let's walk." After we took a dozen steps, he said, "When we arrived in Montego Bay, I was doing some surveillance, as you suspected."

I didn't say a word, so he continued, "Last night's call was from Neil. He flew in yesterday evening. We went to Flankers, got someone out, and he left with Neil last night."

After chewing that over for a few seconds, I looked up at him. "How frequently do you go in to rescue people?"

"Once or twice a month." He tipped his head slightly. "As the need arises."

I tugged his arm and he stopped. "What you're telling me is that anything could have happened to you last night, and I wouldn't have known where you were."

He had the grace to look sheepish. "I'm sorry about that. I've gotten so used to keeping things confidential that it's hard for me to open up to anyone."

"If you trusted me, you would have told me what you were doing a long time ago."

His arm slipped around me and I allowed him to hug me. "You're half right. It's not that I didn't trust you. I guess I thought you wouldn't be able to handle knowing I was in danger half the time we were apart."

I pulled him under the shade of some palm trees. "How long have you been doing this?"

Something shifted in his gaze and he said, "More than a decade."

"What would make you put your life at risk time after time?"

He smiled and assumed a rueful expression. "I wouldn't quite put it that way. I'm an expert at what I do."

A sly grin tugged at my lips. "Is that why you're trying to hide the fact that you're injured?"

Roger gave me a side-eye. "Even veterans in this field are hurt sometimes." He frowned, then added, "I started rescuing people shortly after I lost Rosalie. Could be I had a death wish. Who knows?" He pulled in a deep breath and stroked my arm. "After a while, extracting people became something to do alongside business. If I could make families happy by bringing home their loved ones, I'd add more meaning to my life. That was my rationale for continuing."

He searched my eyes, then said, "I hope you didn't think I was smuggling drugs or anything like that."

I remembered one of my conversations with Khalila when I inferred exactly that, but I wasn't about to tell him.

"And speaking about trust," he continued, "if *you* trusted *me,* you'd have waited for me to come back."

When I gave him a disbelieving look, Roger gripped me by both shoulders. "I've made many mistakes where you're concerned, but I don't want to lose you. Woman, you mean more to me than my own life."

His words weakened me, but I wasn't going to cave and forget how he'd abandoned *us* last night without much of an explanation. "I've already assumed that every time you skipped out on our dates, and when you were in Jamaica a while back...you were 'extracting' people."

Aside from a slight widening of the eyes, Roger didn't react.

I pursed my lips, then admitted, "I accidentally heard you and Doug talking after Zane's christening."

He nodded in acknowledgment of my explanation and released me. "These jobs come up at a moment's notice. Rarely longer than that."

After a thorough probing of his eyes for the truth, I asked, "And you're saying that's what happened last night?"

"You were there when the call came in."

My heart raced as I prepared to quiz him. "So how did that go? Tell me what happens when you do a job, and while you're at it, what happened to your shoulder?"

He put a few inches between us, but his voice was gentle when he said, "You're asking for a lot of information."

"Yeah, because the other day you promised to tell me *everything*."

Roger flinched, then shoved his hands in his pockets. He spoke about where he'd been in the last twelve hours and what he'd done. My attention strayed to his shoulder when he mentioned getting shot, and I gently laid my hand over the imprint of the bandage under his shirt. I didn't ask any more questions, but his revelation made sense of the many times he'd disappeared with little to no notice, giving me the impression that he was unreliable. All those times, he'd been saving lives. This new information gave me much to consider.

"So," he said, his expression earnest. "D'you think you can deal with all that?"

I tipped my head toward the sky and the canopy of leaves above, knowing I'd need more time to think about all the implications. But Roger had gotten to the deepest part of me by being up front about his feelings. I slipped my hand into his. "It's not an ideal situation, but you were doing it long before you met me, and you're still in one piece...mostly, so I might be able to live with it for now."

He cupped my cheek and pecked my lips, then rested his forehead against mine. "Thank you."

We continued walking, sticking close to the shade. Roger was quiet for a long time. Finally, he said, "I've wanted to ask you about this guy, Marcus. Since he dropped back on your radar, and you've had time to think, are you still okay with us?"

"Of course, I am, silly. I was a different person when I fell in love with Marcus." I met Roger's eyes. "And how exactly did you two meet?"

After Roger supplied an explanation, I said, "That's quite a coincidence."

"Agreed, but life is like that. We'll never be able to explain or understand why some incidents unfold the way they do."

With my attention fixed on the powdery sand in front of me, I inhaled and continued, surprised to find that the history I'd bottled up for so many years no longer tasted bitter on my tongue. The fact that I could speak frankly with Roger about my heartbreak told me everything I needed to know.

"Marcus and I believed we could handle anything, until we lost our little girl." Along with my words and my sigh, I released Marcus from my bitterness and absolved myself of blame. "He didn't know how to comfort me, and I didn't know how to deal with feeling like a failure. We couldn't see eye to eye on anything and one day, he got on a plane and left. He didn't tell me where he was going. The way he left shattered something inside me that stayed broken for years."

Aside from gripping my hand too tight and muttering to himself, Roger didn't interrupt. When my explanation tapered off, he scooped me into his body and buried his face in my neck. His lips trailed over my skin until they met mine. My mouth opened and I welcomed him. As our tongues mated to a slow and sensuous rhythm, Roger's body responded and he held me tighter.

My arms closed around his waist and we continued feeding on each other as if we'd been apart for months instead of hours. When we separated, Roger continued dropping kisses at the corners of my mouth and whispering endearments.

"I'm perfectly okay. It's been a while." I slipped my arms down to his chest and teased him. "Since we got together, you've kinda made my life better with your special appearances."

"I've been special all my life," Roger announced.

When I glared at him, Roger laughed. "And by the way, my reaction to you had nothing to do with sympathy or me trying to comfort you."

He was lying through his teeth but I didn't contradict him. Roger couldn't know what I saw in his eyes. The emotion in his brought tears to mine. This man had changed something in me. The urge to run away from anything resembling commitment had left me, and if Roger had it in mind to ask me to be one half of his tomorrow, I wouldn't hesitate to say yes.

When he spoke, I wasn't ready for what he asked, "What do you want more than anything else?"

I tipped my head to one side and looked up at him. "Why?"

His thumb traced the line of my cheek. "I just want you to be happy. I can't make that a reality unless I know what you want or need."

I blinked and the sand shimmered and dissolved in my tears. "I don't know that I need anything special to be happy. Being in the same space with you has been more than enough. And for the future, I need you to be honest with me about *everything*."

He pressed a soft kiss to my ear, then spoke into it. "Yes. That's a promise."

After nipping my lobe, Roger said, "There's something I want to know. I meant to ask you at the apartment that night, but we got distracted."

"What's that?"

One hand stroked my hair and he maintained eye contact. "I've been wondering how you found me at the apartment when I never told you the address, and I'm pretty sure Doug didn't either."

Tapping his chest, I quipped, "Let's just say I'm resourceful."

With both brows raised, he said, "Did you mention honesty a moment ago?"

"Hmmm. I've been reading your tags, okay?" I huffed. "What else was I supposed to do when you refused to level with me? I hope you've learned a lesson. We'll always be at odds if you keep going into Secret Squirrel mode."

He laughed, then a slow, sexy smile widened his lips. "Does that mean if I want to make our arrangement permanent, you won't disappear on me?"

My eyes filled again, and the tears ran down my cheeks. With both arms, I circled his neck. "I've done enough running in my life. Maybe it's time to see what love looks like up close."

Roger lifted my chin and touched his lips to mine. "I'm not afraid to say I love you. I figured knowing how I feel about you would prevent you from running again."

"It did. Thank you for having the courage to show me what was on your heart." I held his head between my hands and looked him in the eyes. "I don't want you to doubt that I love you, too. I think that's part of the reason your secrets bothered me so much. If you were hiding parts of your life, then it meant you weren't committed to us."

"I didn't see it like that. I was wrong. Please forgive me." His mouth covered mine and we shared another searing kiss.

When I caught my breath, I spoke against his lips. "About keeping me happy. There is one thing you could do. I wanted to go horseback riding and try the ATV wilderness adventure, but I guess it will keep for another time."

"That's two, but we can do both the next time we're here."

The tenderness in his eyes made my heart ache. I looked away, but he turned my head with a finger under my chin. "Anything you want, I'll do my best to make it happen."

I slipped my hand into his as we walked past tourists sunning themselves on the sand. When we came to a thatch umbrella that hadn't been claimed by anyone, I pulled him underneath it and wrapped my arms around him. "I have one more question for you."

Roger pecked my forehead. "Ask away, Queen Corinne."

"Um. Can I come with you on one of your rescues? You know, be part of the action?"

Roger's indulgent gaze turned analytical, then pensive.

I pulled back my head, sensing I might not get the answer I wanted. "You did say you were willing to keep me happy."

"Never doubt that's exactly what I intend to do as long as we live."

"So, can I come the next time you do an extraction?"

This time, his answer was swift. "Hell, no."

"Roger!"

He silenced me by pulling me to his chest and sealing my mouth to his. Roger knew exactly what he was doing because the gentle assault of his tongue left me weak-kneed. His breath brushed my ear and he whispered, "Even if you *could* help me on a mission, I'd still love you enough to refuse to put your life in danger. My answer to that question will always be no."

I huffed and laid my head on his chest. "If you say so."

"I'm serious, Corinne."

My only answer was a smirk. In truth, I'd have been surprised if he said yes. As I thought about all the fun adventures we could have together and the places we could visit, I hugged him tighter. My life had needed shaking up, and Roger had been the man to do it. Too bad I'd taken this long to recognize that I still needed healing. My thoughts went on hold when Roger trailed a path under my ear with his tongue. "But if you're game for some excitement later this evening ..."

I leaned into him, relishing what the rest of the day would bring. My response captured not only what I felt in the moment, but what I hoped for in the future. "Always."

other books by j.l. campbell

Romantic Suspense (Island Adventure Series)

Anya's Wish

Chasing Anya

Contraband

Taming Celeste

Grudge

Hardware

Kings of the Castle

King of Evanston (Kings of the Castle)

Knight of Paradise Island (Knights of the Castle)

Queen of Kingston (Queens of the Castle)

New Adult

Perfection

Fixation

Persuasion

Women's Fiction

A Baker's Dozen-13 Steps to Distraction (novella)

Dissolution

Distraction

Retribution

Absolution

The Thick of Things

The Heart of Things

The Pain of Things

Inspirational Fiction

DNA

Sacrifice

Dominic' Pride

Inspirational Non-Fiction

Vision: Aligning With God's Purpose For Your Life

Young Adult

Christine's Odyssey

Saving Sam

Short Story Collections

Don't Get Mad...Get Even (free)

Don't Get Mad...Get Even: Kicked to the Kerb

Contemporary Romance

The Short Game

The Long Game

The Spice of Life

The Blind Shot

The Hole-in-One

Contemporary Romance (Sweet Holiday Series)

The Vet's Christmas Pet

The Vet's Valentine Gift

The Vet's Secret Wish

Sold!

Cupid's Gift

Blindsided

Paranormal Romance

Phantasm

about the author

National Bestselling Author, J.L. Campbell, writes contemporary, paranormal, and sweet romance, romantic suspense, inspirational and women's fiction, as well as new and young adult novels.

Campbell, who hails from Jamaica, has penned over forty books. She is a certified editor, and book coach.

When she's not writing, Campbell adds to her extensive collection of photos featuring Jamaica's natural beauty.

contact

FB Fan Page - https://www.facebook.com/jlcampbellwrites/
BookBub - https://www.bookbub.com/authors/j-l-campbell
Twitter - https://twitter.com/JL_Campbell
Instagram - https://www.instagram.com/jl.campbell/
Newsletter - bit.ly/JLCampbellsNewsletter
Goodreads - https//www.goodreads.com/jlcampbell
Pinterest - https://www.pinterest.com/thewriterssuite
Website - https://www.joylcampbell.com
Clubhouse - http://www.clubhouse.com/@jl_campbell
Sociatap - https://sociatap.com/JL_Campbell/

Lightning Source UK Ltd.
Milton Keynes UK
UKHW011124160223
417122UK00006B/573